"I love that kid so much— so damn much—"

Logan said, "that the thought of losing her just…"

A hard, hot lump formed in Whitney's throat. God knows, she'd do anything for Logan Monroe. All he had to do was ask.

"I'll find a replacement for the special teddy bear your little foster daughter lost," she said. "I promise."

"Can you believe I'm looking high and low for a teddy bear?" Logan asked. "Sometimes I think it would be easier just to find myself a wife. Maybe *that* would make the adoption caseworker happy."

Whitney stared into Logan's blue eyes, and the most unimaginable, awesome thought crossed her mind. She had to bite her lip, and her cheeks ached from trying not to smile as she considered offering herself up as the sacrificial lamb.

But could she bring herself to say it? Could she actually…propose?

Dear Reader,

September is here again, bringing the end of summer—but not the end of relaxing hours spent with a good book. This month Silhouette brings you six new Romance novels that will fill your leisure hours with pleasure. And don't forget to see how Silhouette Books makes you a star!

First, Myrna Mackenzie continues the popular MAITLAND MATERNITY series with *A Very Special Delivery,* when Laura Maitland is swept off her feet on the way to the delivery room! Then we're off to DESTINY, TEXAS, where, in *This Kiss,* a former plain Jane returns home to teach the class heartthrob a thing or two about chemistry. Don't miss this second installment of Teresa Southwick's exciting series. Next, in *Cinderella After Midnight,* the first of Lilian Darcy's charming trilogy THE CINDERELLA CONSPIRACY, we go to a ball with "Lady Catrina"—who hasn't bargained on a handsome millionaire seeing through her disguise....

Whitney Bloom's dreams come true in DeAnna Talcott's *Marrying for a Mom,* when she marries the man she loves— even if only to keep custody of his daughter. In *Wed by a Will,* the conclusion of THE WEDDING LEGACY, reader favorite Cara Colter brings together a new family—and reunites us with other members. Then, a prim and proper businesswoman finds she wants a lot more from the carpenter who's remodeling her house than watertight windows in Gail Martin's delightful *Her Secret Longing.*

Be sure to return next month for Stella Bagwell's conclusion to MAITLAND MATERNITY and the start of a brand-new continuity—HAVING THE BOSS'S BABY! Beloved author Judy Christenberry launches this wonderful series with *When the Lights Went Out...* Don't miss any of next month's wonderful tales.

Happy reading!

Mary-Theresa Hussey

Mary-Theresa Hussey
Senior Editor

Please address questions and book requests to:
Silhouette Reader Service
U.S.: 3010 Walden Ave., P.O. Box 1325, Buffalo, NY 14269
Canadian: P.O. Box 609, Fort Erie, Ont. L2A 5X3

Marrying for a Mom

DeAnna TALCOTT

SILHOUETTE *Romance*®

Published by Silhouette Books

America's Publisher of Contemporary Romance

Dedicated to the memory of Jeanne Breaugh, and the
LaSenorita bunch she mentored—Lisa, Joyce, Dickee,
Lana, Diane and Marjorie. They labor over words, plots
and GMC while taking a few sneaky time-outs
to turn down the volume of the mariachi music.

 SILHOUETTE BOOKS

ISBN 0-373-19543-5

MARRYING FOR A MOM

Copyright © 2001 by DeAnna Talcott

Visit Silhouette at www.eHarlequin.com

Printed in U.S.A.

Books by DeAnna Talcott

Silhouette Romance

The Cowboy and the Christmas Tree #1125
The Bachelor and the Bassinet #1189
To Wed Again? #1206
The Triplet's Wedding Wish #1370
Marrying for a Mom #1543

DeANNA TALCOTT

grew up in rural Nebraska, where her love of reading was fostered in a one-room school. It was there she first dreamed of writing the kinds of books that would touch people's hearts. Her dream became a reality when not one, but two of her Silhouette Romance novels won Readers' Choice Awards. Those books also earned her a slot as a *Romantic Times Magazine* nominee, while *The Bachelor and the Bassinet* was named as one of *Romantic Times Magazine*'s Top Picks.

DeAnna claims that a retired husband, three children, two dogs and a matching pair of alley cats make her life in mid-Michigan particularly interesting. When not writing, or talking about writing, she scrounges in flea markets to indulge #1 son's quest for vintage toys, relaxes at #2 son's Eastern Michigan football and baseball games, and insists, to her daughter, that two cats simply do not need to multiply!

SILHOUETTE MAKES YOU A STAR!
Feel like a star with Silhouette.
Look for the exciting details of our new contest
inside all of these fabulous Silhouette novels:

Chapter One

Whitney Bloom paused, then reached over to readjust Byron's handcrafted sweater. Byron, Whitney's favorite teddy bear, occupied the spot next to the cash register in her specialty store, Teddy Bear Heaven. Like a silent partner, he'd spent the last six years listening to all her hopes and dreams, and commiserating with all her disappointments.

"You know what?" she whispered to Byron. "If we work our fingers to the bone this summer, we could be solvent in six months." Levering her elbows against the counter, she threaded her ankles around the stool rungs and raised slightly off the wooden stool she sat on. She picked up another bolt, convinced she'd have the teddy bear-size park bench assembled in record time. "I predict—" she paused for dramatic effect, and waved the screwdriver "—that there will be a bumper crop of tourists in Melville this summer, and every one will want—no, *need*—a teddy bear to take home to their kids. In fact, right at this very minute, someone, somewhere, is thinking that what they really need is a teddy bear to cuddle and love."

The bell over the front door tinkled. Whitney looked up,

astonished to think her prediction had come true, and promptly lost her balance. The bolt she had just picked up skittered across the wide plank flooring.

From across the room, and with the sun at his back, a man's silhouette reached over the hardwood flooring, nearly to the glass case she was sitting behind. As he stepped into her showroom, Whitney recognized the wide shoulders and lean arms, the tapered waist and muscular thighs.

Logan Monroe.

Two heartbeats of dead silence followed, and a million uninvited memories made Whitney's knees buckle.

Suddenly her heart did a little tap dance, just as it did every time she saw him. The heel-toe combination made her go weak all over. Then, Logan flashed her the famous Monroe smile—the same one the *Melville Post* routinely printed in the Sunday edition of the want ads. The copy beneath his photo never changed, and she should know because she read it faithfully: Logan Monroe, Realtor, specializing in vacation properties for Melville, Lake Justice and the southeastern Tennessee area.

Whitney's composure plummeted. Her stomach turned inside out. Her mouth went dry and her heart pounded. Whitney hadn't seen Logan in twelve years; saying she was tongue-tied would be an understatement.

"Hey, sorry about that," Logan said easily, without really looking at her. When he doubled over to pick the bolt up off the floor, Whitney stared at the smooth arc of his shoulders, aware his clothes looked loose on him, as if he'd lost a little weight. "I didn't mean to startle you." He sidestepped the child-size teddy bear table and chair set that was in the middle of the crowded room, and laid the bolt on the counter.

Whitney gazed at it, half-afraid to pick it up for fear she would drop it all over again. The muscles in her shoulders constricted.

Logan didn't really look at her, his gaze was fixed on

the shelves behind her, where the expensive collector bears and one-of-a-kinds were housed. "I'm looking for a bear."

With only six feet between them, Whitney realized Logan still looked the same. Only older. Better.

He still carried his six-foot-four frame with the same self-confidence. His hair—one shade darker than tobacco—was now sheared straight, and closely cropped. His angular face and thick jaw complemented brows that were perfectly matched slashes over cobalt eyes. His nose was narrow at the bridge, his nostrils, wide and thick. His mouth was full, and had a tendency to twitch when amused.

"Then you've come to the right place," Whitney managed to say as Logan started moving around the counter.

He stopped, turning on his heel. From behind a rack of teddy bear barrettes and hair clips, Logan shimmied a glance in her direction.

Whitney noted the faint smile lines fanning from the corners of his eyes and shivered. He was despicably good-looking, that's what he was. Despicably good-looking.

"Whitney…?" he said as a flicker of recognition sparked behind his eyes. His mouth had worked its way around her name, whispering it softly, as if in disbelief. "Oh, my God, Whit…is it you?"

She nodded slowly, her breath shallow. She briefly debated whether she should offer up an apology for what had happened all those years ago or just forget it. She wondered how much he remembered.

"Damn. Why didn't you say something?"

She guiltily lifted both shoulders. "I don't know. When you came in the door, I didn't think you'd ever look at me. Really look, I mean. And then I didn't know if I should… because…"

"Whitney. C'mon," he chided. Then he took her in. From the top of her professionally highlighted, chin-length cut, to the gold bracelet on her wrist, and the pearl studs in her ears. His gaze lingered on the understated elegance of her sweater and matching slacks before his jaw slid off center. "I'm looking," he said. "And I mean really, really looking," he emphasized.

Whitney's smile grew more tentative. "It's been a long time, Logan."

"It has. Too long, Whit."

Still, the uncertainty of their past hung between them. Harsh words, threats, and accusations had all been rolled up into their last goodbye. It had been a nasty scene. Logan had been outraged, Whitney defensive. To make matters worse, her ex-husband had offered up a dozen feeble excuses as to why Logan's books didn't balance and his petty cash was missing. It had been the only time Whitney had ever heard Logan raise his voice; it had been the only time Whitney had ever let anyone but Gram see her cry.

They both stood there, awkwardly, both unsure of what to say.

"Hey, look—"

"I always wanted to—"

They both laughed self-consciously, both biting back apologies.

"Okay. This is crazy. Look. I feel like I should hug you or something…" He lifted his arms, awkwardly, as if he didn't know the correct protocol for when old friends, who were no longer friends, let time patch up their differences.

He glanced down at the glass counter standing between them.

For a second, a long-held fantasy went winging through Whitney's head. Logan, a superhero, would leap over the barriers that separated them, then sweep her into his arms. *Faster than a speeding bullet, more powerful than a locomotive.* He could fix anything, he could move mountains, he could mend hearts.

Shaking herself free of the daydream, Whitney took it upon herself to make something happen: she slid from the stool and extended her hand.

For a moment, everything seemed disjointed. Like pieces that were trying to fit back together again. Her gold bracelet glittered beneath the overhead fluorescent lighting, and her French manicured nails made her fingers appear long and slender and cultured.

They both knew she wasn't. Cultured, that is. In Melville, she'd been raised on the "other" side of the tracks.

His hand reached for hers. The bones in his wrist were thick, his knuckles dimpled. The smattering of dark hair over the back of his hand was sexy, evoking powerful images of strength and wealth and confidence.

They had no business joining hands—and she had no business feeling the way she did about him. Especially after everything that had happened.

"Whitney." Logan clasped her fingers, then covered the back of her hand with his palm as she came around the counter. A liquid warmth spread through her, convincing her the past was forgotten, that he was genuinely pleased to see her. "You look—" his gaze slipped down her front, all the way to her skimmers "—great." When he lifted his eyes, their gaze caught and held. "Wonderful," he amended. "Absolutely, positively stunning."

Whitney's smile softened, and she felt a rush of heat, from the inside out.

"You know," he reminded, "we've got a lot of history together."

"And not all of it good." She couldn't help herself, the truth had to come out.

Logan grimaced, then gave her fingers a light squeeze before reluctantly loosening them. "Hey. Remember the time we connected on that pitching mound at the company picnic, and my watch did a number on your chin?" he asked, intentionally changing the subject.

Her forefinger automatically flicked over the spot. "How could I forget three stitches and a tetanus?"

He critically eyed the tiny white scar, and his hands moved as if they had a will of their own, to capture her jaw between thumb and forefinger, and angle the spot closer for his inspection. "I practically mowed you down, going after that fly ball.'' Logan distinctly remembered how she'd crumpled beneath him, all soft, in a flurry of fighting limbs. The scent of leather gloves and dirt and diamond dust, and the *thwunk* as her chin connected with his wrist. But the worst was, after they'd collided, her husband yanked her up off the ground, dusted her off and told Logan not to worry, no damage. He'd had to remind himself to forget it, to tell himself it was none of his business, that she was married and that she belonged to someone else. Then he'd had to beat back the regrets. "The insurance cover three stitches and a tetanus?"

Whitney started to shake her head, but stopped, not wanting to break from his touch. "It doesn't matter. It was a long time ago."

The intensity of his blue gaze held her, as if he were trying to absorb her and look into her soul. A tremulous anxiety clutched Whitney, making her falter, making her breathing erratic.

"Logan?" she finally whispered.

"It…um…it left a mark," he murmured, refocusing on her chin, as his thumb gently flicked over the tiny cleft.

"It barely shows."

His fingers fell away. "Still…the physical evidence remains. We've had more brushes with fate than any two people should have to endure."

The moment—and the references—were awkward.

Whitney's smile thinned. Logan deftly changed the subject. Again.

"Damn, I've driven by this place a hundred times. I can't believe you own it."

"Lease it," Whitney qualified.

"So…" he said softly, considering. "You're the teddy bear lady."

Whitney tipped her head. "Please. Don't you dare say it's cute. I love it, but it's a business and it pays the bills. I have every kind and type of teddy bear you could ever imagine."

"I guess you do." Logan swept the room with an all-inclusive look. It was jam-packed with teddy bears. Teddy bear toothbrushes swung on a revolving display, and teddy bear books were wedged on teddy bear bookshelves. There were teddy bear clocks, jewelry, stationery and stickers. Teddy bear erasers, pencils, pens and rulers. Framed prints, and bath accessories. Even shower curtains, regular curtains, blankets and rugs. He chuckled, his smile riding a tad bit higher on the left. "But I never intended to say 'cute.' I'm impressed. It's a great concept. When I look around, I'm inclined to buy the store out."

"What? And reduce my inventory?" she asked dryly.

"Whitney, this place is great. And it's just like you to think of something this clever."

The praise startled Whitney, putting a pink flush in her cheeks.

"What?" he asked, mimicking her. "Am I embarrassing you?" He didn't wait for an answer. "I mean it. You were the one who always came up with the most creative ideas in high school. You were the one with the interesting slant on life."

"Out of necessity."

"Right. Like the time you suggested that instead of having a formal banquet for the National Honor Society, we have a picnic? That was the best day ever, and you were responsible for it. A whole day at the beach, playing Frisbee, and volleyball, and splashing around."

A shred of guilt crept into Whitney's conscience; she'd suggested the idea because she didn't have the twenty-five dollars for the banquet ticket.

"And what about that idea you had for prom? Fifties night at the Peppermint Lounge? We got by decorating with peppermint sticks, borrowed a jukebox and used the rest of the money in the treasury for catering the senior banquet so it didn't cost any of us a cent." A second guilty flush prickled over the back of Whitney's neck. She'd intended to go, and wear an old fifties formal Gram had tucked away

in the attic. "And to top it off," he went on, "after you
came up with the idea, you never even went to the prom.
I specifically went looking for you, to con you out of one
dance."

Whitney shrugged, her smile tight as she minimized the
details. "Gram's health was kind of up and down just
then."

Logan sobered. "You always did have a lot of responsibility looking after her."

"Logan. She was looking after *me*."

"I think," he said slowly, "you looked after each
other." He chuckled, as another memory hit him. "Your
gram was something else, though. I'll never forget how she
rode all over Melville on that three-wheel bike of hers."

Whitney shifted uncomfortably; Gram had ridden a bi-
cycle because they couldn't afford a car. The truth was,
Whitney and Logan had hung out with different crowds,
and had literally been from opposite sides of the have/have-
not world.

Logan had lived in a big house on the hill, and spent his
summers tanning at the country club. His parents owned
several car dealerships, and made sure their only son never
lacked for a thing. He'd loved playing the part of the big,
brash jock, and had run around Melville in a brand-new
sports car, making sure he was noticed on every intersection by revving his engine and waving at all the girls.

Whitney, raised by her grandmother, had lived in a
rented bungalow just off of Main. It was a dilapidated little
house, with a barren scrap of a front yard, and a painted
tractor tire that held a few scraggly petunias. Whitney never
invited friends in because they stared at the black spots on
the linoleum, the water rings on the drop ceiling, and the
peeling wallpaper in the front room. Still, she loved Gram
dearly, and it would have cut her to the quick to have anyone say Gram hadn't provided for her.

Without warning, Logan reached across her, to skim the

tiny teddy bear charm from around her neck and balance it on the pad of his forefinger. The fine gold chain swayed beneath her chin, pulling slightly.

"Just like this shop…" he said, catching Whitney's eye. This close, the sloe-dark color on her eyelids was fascinating. He leaned closer, thinking she smelled like a crazy mixture of vanilla and fabric softener. The links in the necklace, draped over the hollow of her throat, rolled up and down with every breath she took. "Details. Perfect details, Whit. Only you could pull this off."

"Maybe. But teddy bears aren't as fancy as real estate, or owning car dealerships or a marina, so—"

"No," he said quickly, letting the teddy bear charm fall from the tip of his finger. "It fits. Only you could do something this memorable. Something that would touch people and put a soft spot in their heart."

Whitney shuddered. Matters of the heart were the last thing she wanted to discuss. Especially with Logan Monroe. "Okay, Logan," she said unsteadily, "I know you didn't come in here to give me warm fuzzies, and admire my shop. What's up?"

Logan's mouth quirked, but the light in his eyes slowly faded. "I came in here to replace a teddy bear," he said, his tone subtly changing. "I should have done it months ago, but…hey, look," he went on, his voice suddenly lifting, "I want to show you something. In fact, I'm *proud* to show you this little something…." Logan reached in his back pocket and pulled out his wallet, flipping through the plastic windows. On the opposite side, a sliver of plastic showed: American Express Platinum.

Whitney blanched, thinking how some things—even a piece of plastic—can put you in your place. In her wallet, she carried only one low-limit credit card to the local discount store. It had been all she could do to get this store off the ground, and every cent she'd had she put back into the business. For a year, she'd slept on a rollaway in the back room and cooked on a hot plate.

"Here," he announced, pausing at the photo of a little girl perched on a wicker rocker. Her legs were crossed at the ankles, and in her hands, and propped over her shoulder, an exquisite lace parasol framed the tangle of flaxen curls cascading over her shoulders. "I had this taken for my wife two years ago. For Mother's Day."

Whitney couldn't breathe. "Your daughter?" she said numbly. She knew Logan had married a girl from Memphis, but she hadn't known they'd had a child.

"My foster daughter."

"The bear's for her," Whitney guessed, vaguely hearing his clarification.

He nodded. "See?" he said. "That's the bear she always used to carry around. The photographer propped it against the chair because Amanda insisted it had to be in the picture. She never went anywhere without it."

Amanda. Her name was Amanda.

"She's darling, Logan."

His smile was full and proud. "Thanks. And I want a teddy bear just like that."

Whitney started, and swiveled toward Logan. "That may not be possible," she warned before squinting back at the photo. She wasn't able to make out any real details, but there were thousands of styles of teddy bears, and hundreds of manufacturers with their own distinctive signature.

"I don't think it was very unusual, probably the dime-store variety, but I want the exact same thing." He paused, before going on to explain, "She lost it...the day my wife died."

Whitney slowly lifted her eyes, pinning him. She tried to detect his grief, but only saw carefully veiled shadows in his faintly lined face. "I'm so sorry, Logan...about your wife. I should have offered my condolences first, before we started talking. The moment you walked in the door, I should have said..."

He held up a hand, stopping her. "No, that's okay. Two more months and it'll be a year. I'm getting used to it. No one could have predicted an aneurysm, not in someone that young… It was a shock, but…I don't talk about it much.''

''Still…I should have sent a card.''

An uncomfortable second of silence slipped away.

''Why didn't you?'' he asked bluntly after a moment.

''I—I didn't know if you'd want to hear from me,'' she said honestly.

He stared at her, as if measuring his response before uttering it. ''Whitney. Forget it. The thing with your husband has been over with for a long time.''

''My ex-husband,'' she said quietly.

The wallet he held dropped a fraction of an inch. ''Oh? I always wondered. I just didn't think it would be good to—you know…'' He didn't say it, but she knew. It wouldn't be a good idea to fraternize in any way, shape, or form with the wife of a small town, small time crook. Especially after you threatened to press charges for dipping into the petty cash.

''I found out you weren't the first employer he took advantage of. He worked at the grocery and filched steaks from the freezer. He worked at the gas station and helped himself to gas from the pumps.''

''If I could have avoided firing him, I would have, Whitney.''

''I know that.''

''You don't sound convinced.''

She shrugged. ''This is hard for me, Logan. You do me a favor by offering him a job, and then he repays you by letting a few twenties attach themselves to his fingers.''

''It was a long time ago, Whit,'' he said brusquely. ''We'd both be better off to put it in the past. In the whole scheme of things it really isn't important.''

Right. One deplorable incident. Gone, but not entirely forgotten.

Whitney took a deep, cleansing breath, reminding herself that whatever followed between her and Logan was business, and business only. "So," she said, "tell me about this bear."

He pulled the photo back into their line of vision. "I thought maybe you might have something…in the store…"

Whitney shook her head. She should have studied the bear, but instead her gaze was drawn to the child. "I don't think so. But we can look. I'll flip over the Closed sign and, even if it takes all night, you can go through my inventory."

That wheedled a small, sad smile from him. He slowly closed the wallet, as if considering her offer.

"She's a darling little girl, Logan," Whitney said carefully. "I had no idea you were a daddy."

"Yeah. We got her when she was about three years old. So I honestly think of her as my daughter. I love her as if—as if—" Logan's voice dried up, and he suddenly choked over the sentence he couldn't bring himself to say.

As if she were your daughter, Whitney silently finished for him. She studied him, fascinated. For a devil-may-care personality, he had the kindest heart. Always had. "Logan?" she queried, summoning the courage to touch him, to lay her hand on his forearm. "What is it?"

Logan's eyes closed, shutting her out of his pain. He twisted slightly at the waist, and her hand dropped away, as he put the wallet back into his pocket. "We were in the process of adopting her, but there was a lot of red tape. It took us a long time to find the biological parents and when we located them, the father agreed to relinquish his rights—but the mother kept changing her mind. Then, last year, the mother finally signed away her rights and the adoption was in the final stages. But then Jill died, leaving me as a single father, and now the agency is stalling. The caseworker says my company takes too much of my time, and that they feel it's in Amanda's best interest to be raised in a two-parent household. She told me last week they have a couple who inquired about adopting an older child, preferably a girl. She left me with the feeling that they could remove

Amanda from the house. Maybe within the next few weeks.''

Whitney went limp all over. She knew what is was like to be jerked out of one home and dropped into another. Her mother had experimented with boyfriends, and communes, and middle-of-the-night flights from unpaid landlords and unfortunate affairs. ''Oh, Logan, I'm so sorry. If there's anything I can do….''

''You can. Help me get this bear for Amanda before they take her away. I don't want her to think I'm abandoning *her*. Hell, I'd do anything to keep her.''

''Does she have any idea?''

Logan shook his head. ''The social worker's intimated things to her, suggested that maybe she would like another house, with a new mommy…''

Whitney groaned, the small of her back sinking against the counter. ''No. Tell me she didn't say that?''

''Yeah,'' he said grimly. ''She did. I suppose she meant well. But Amanda will be traumatized if they take her away. She's too young to remember her life prior to living with us. We're all she's ever known.''

Whitney's vision blurred. She vividly remembered a grocery sack full of clothes, a nonchalant goodbye and a pat on the head from her mother.

''Sure, as a single dad, I've had a few mishaps along the way,'' he confided. ''But I've learned from them. I've even learned how to make fifteen nutritious variations of canned spaghetti.''

''Nutritious canned spaghetti?'' She couldn't help it— she laughed.

He lifted an apologetic shoulder. ''On the food chain, it's one notch above tuna, or peanut butter and jelly sandwiches.''

Whitney had to bite her bottom lip. Her cheeks ached from trying not to smile. Her mother had never even cared enough to even open a can of tuna, let alone slap peanut butter on a slice of bread.

"Whitney, listen to me," he said earnestly. "If I replace that bear, and Amanda's taken away, it'll give her a connection to something she loved. She needs to know that no matter what happens, I'm there for her. I love that kid so much—so damn much—that the thought of losing her, just...."

A hot, hard lump swelled in Whitney's throat; she willed her response to be firm, not shaky. God knows, she'd do anything for Logan. All he had to do was ask. "I can tell you right now I don't have anything like it in the store. But I'll find it," Whitney said. "I promise."

"Can you believe this? Can you believe I'm looking for a teddy bear?" he asked humorlessly. "Sometimes I think it would just be easier to find myself a wife. Maybe *that* would make the caseworker happy."

Whitney stared into the depths of his ice-blue eyes and the most unimaginable thought crossed her mind. She just couldn't bring herself to say it. Suddenly she was paralyzed by the awesomeness of it all.

She vaguely considered offering herself up as the sacrificial lamb.

"Whitney?"

A second slipped away.

"Yes, Logan?"

"Thank you," he said simply. "For you to do this, especially after everything that's happened...well, it makes me realize I overlooked something very special in high school."

The expression of gratitude took her breath away. His praise was so unexpected. As teenagers, they had shared a few laughs, the same row of seats in study hall, and, on Senior Skip Day, one near kiss...something that, in later years, she'd silently regretted as her "one near miss." Later, when Logan offered her ex a job, and he'd so badly messed that up, she had apologized repeatedly, hoping to redeem herself in Logan's eyes. But Logan had been young and angry, and he'd stalked away.

After years of beating herself up over that horrific parting it seemed inconceivable that all she had to do to make things better was find a teddy bear. It was a small price to pay to be able to put the matter to rest, and get the man and the memories out of her mind.

Still, Whitney would never know what prompted her to say what she did next, maybe it was because she was a new woman and she had come of age, and into her own. She had the security, and the confidence to dare to remind him. "Not something," she corrected quietly. "*Someone*. You overlooked someone. Someone like me."

Chapter Two

Logan leaned back, as far as his leather desk chair would allow, and pinched the bridge of his nose. It had been a long, wearisome day. He was bone-tired and the house looked like a tornado had struck. Four hours ago, his third housekeeper quit to take care of her grandchildren in California, and he was at his wit's end.

All he'd asked of the woman was to supervise Amanda after school and put a hot meal on the table. She'd accepted his generous paycheck, and done exactly that and no more. The laundry was piled up to the rafters, the sink was overflowing with dirty dishes and the carpets reminded him of one giant lint trap. Amanda had taken to writing her name on the TV screen, and playing tic-tac-toe in the dust on the coffee table. Games and toys, and shoes and socks were scattered in every room in the house, and the counters were a hodgepodge of newspapers, magazines, advertisements and old mail.

How had Jill done it? She'd managed to get Amanda to school on time, and he never remembered her scrambling to find a matching pair of shoes or digging through the couch cushions for lunch money.

This was the worst it had been. The worst.

He couldn't ask his mom to fill in again. This was their busiest time of year at the marina, and his dad was already making noises about clearing cars off the lot to make room for the new ones that would be coming out.

Talk about being between the devil and the deep blue. His folks had already made it clear that he should give it up, that Amanda was too much responsibility for him right now. On top of everything else, he couldn't bear to hear their "I told you so's." He supposed they were thinking of his best interests, but then, when it came to family, they'd always thought with their heads and not their hearts.

Jill's family had never been pleased they had taken in a foster child. They thought she should have her own children—and pointedly emphasized Amanda was "not really theirs." After Jill passed away, he'd heard from them only once.

What the hell was he going to do?

Deep inside, there were moments he could actually feel his heart ache. The empty feeling he had been carrying around for so long had become fatiguing, making his arms hurt and his head muzzy. He knew one thing: he yearned to laugh again. But if he lost his bid to keep Amanda....

"Dammit. Forget that. I'm not thinking like that. I'm not giving it up." Dragging a hand over his face, Logan flopped forward, letting the chair slip into the upright position. Wedging both elbows on the desk, he absently fingered the cards in his Rolodex.

He'd already called everyone he knew, asking about babysitters. His secretary had given him the name of that place in Nashville that provided nannies, but warned this was the poorest possible time to pursue it; it could take weeks.

There was always Aunt June, the old maid schoolteacher on his dad's side of the family. But Amanda said she smelled like camphor and breath mints, and Logan knew her mind was wandering a little. The last time they visited she'd put the roses in the freezer and displayed a frozen leg of lamb on the table, right between the gold filigree candelabras, as the centerpiece.

He tapped the cards in the Rolodex, as if he, like Houdini, could invoke an answer. Suddenly things became crystal clear to him.

Tomorrow morning he'd make arrangements for the cleaning service to come twice a week. He'd start taking everything to the cleaners. Then he'd call the school and get Amanda back in the after-school program. Until then, he'd just have to cut back his hours, that's all. No big deal, he'd done it before.

But he *had* to get things in order, because he was running out of time. The caseworker from the adoption agency would probably drop in sometime next week. She liked to pop in unannounced, and catch him when everything was in shambles.

Well, this would be a victory for her side.

What a deal. What a raw deal.

If he could just come up with that teddy bear. He'd come to regard the silly thing as a kind of insurance, like an omen, or a talisman that beat back the nasties. But Whitney wasn't optimistic, not about finding it as quickly as he'd hoped.

Whitney. Whitney Thompson Bloom. The name rolled through his mind, inexplicably soothing all the distress and disorder.

He'd been thinking a lot about her lately, and it bothered him because he didn't know why. Probably because he was just so damn obsessed with getting that bear.

She'd changed...yet, it was like the person she'd always been on the inside was coming out. He'd known her as well as anyone in high school, but she'd never let people get too close.

If you looked at Whitney when she didn't know you

were watching, she carried the most vulnerable quality in her eyes. Like she'd been hurt. Deeply hurt. Like she was aching to trust, but she was scared at the same time, too.

He was beginning to understand that feeling.

Three days ago, in her shop, it occurred to him he could lose himself in her eyes. Without glasses, her irises were ginger-dark, and speckled with flecks of delft and daffodil. Striking, gorgeous eyes. But now, he severely reminded himself, with the juggling act he was doing, he couldn't afford to even think about them, let alone be distracted by them.

Whitney flipped through the last manufacturer's catalog, pausing to compare one of their featured bears to the open book on her counter. Then she checked it against the picture Logan had taken from his wallet and left with her. It wasn't the same. Not even close.

She ran a fingernail along the dog-eared corners of the photo, wondering how many times Logan's fingers had traced these same edges. She couldn't get him out of her head. His wholesome, tanned appearance nagged at her— like he made khakis and a sport shirt a dress uniform. Eyes so blue, so insightful and clear, that it made her wonder if a few drops of the Atlantic tinted his gaze. The quizzical lift of his mouth that made him look so kissable.

This was awful. It was terrible.

Thinking so much about Logan made her edgy. It made her wish she was someone she wasn't. It made her reconsider the past, and think about the differences that had kept them apart, and made him unattainable. His money, and her lack of it. His country club membership, and her job bagging groceries and pushing carts at the supermarket. His Camaro and her school bus pass.

How many times had she thought about what he'd said about the prom? Ten? Twenty? She'd stretched the truth on that one. She hadn't gone to the prom because her mom promised to send money for the ticket but decided, on a

whim, to fly to Bangkok instead. There was great airfare
to Bangkok, her mom had written later—a once in a lifetime opportunity. Just like the prom. And Logan had come
looking for a dance—just one—and she wasn't even there.

She was thirty-two years old, for heaven's sake. Why
was she dwelling on this stuff? Pushing the aggravating
memories from her head, Whitney severely reminded herself that she had a life outside the incidents that happened
years ago. She was happy and content with all she'd
achieved. She knew full well that once she found the bear,
her connection to Logan would be severed. He'd go on with
his life; she'd go on with hers.

Her only purpose, she told herself firmly, was to find that
bear—and that was proving to be difficult. She'd browsed
the Internet until four, and still hadn't come up with any
leads. The crazy thing was, the bear wasn't even anything
out of the ordinary.

Yet, to Amanda, she knew it was priceless and unique.
If the child needed something to carry her into the next
phase of her life, Whitney could guarantee a teddy bear
would do it.

After all, Whitney knew firsthand about losing things.
When her mom took off for the last time, the landlord
cleaned out their apartment and put everything in the trash.
Nothing had been salvaged, and her childhood had been
snuffed out in a Dumpster. Whitney had had nightmares
for months afterward, knowing her beloved stuffed animals,
her dolls, her drawings and books, had been thrown away.
Gram had understood her pain, and gone without her ar-
thritis medicine for a whole month so she could buy Whitney a special teddy bear to cuddle and love. That was one
of the reasons she'd started this store, kind of like a living
memorial to her gram.

Reaching for the phone, Whitney punched in the number,
suddenly and inexplicably annoyed with this elusive teddy
bear. She'd find this thing, one way or another.

"Monroe Realty," the receptionist intoned.

"Logan Monroe, please."

The receptionist hesitated before issuing her automatic response. "Mr. Monroe is in a meeting right now, may I take a message?"

"My name is Whitney Bloom, from Teddy Bear Heaven. I have some information he requested. I'll be available until five, and the number is—"

"Oh, Miss Bloom. Just a minute. I think he'd like to take this call. In fact, I know he would. I'll put you right through."

Whitney couldn't beat back her surprise; obviously the receptionist had had her instructions. The pause was momentary.

"Whitney. Hello." Logan's voice was just as mellow, just as resonant as she remembered. Fatigue melted away, and she warmed, remembering how he'd looked, framed by her showroom of teddy bears. He'd purchased three coloring books, markers, a barrette and a pricey dresser set before he'd left, claiming he wanted to make her time worthwhile. "Look, I was just stepping out, but I'm glad you caught me."

"I'm sorry, you've probably got a house to show. I only wanted to tell you there's no good news on this end. I'm beginning to call this the 'un*bear*able teddy bear chase.'"
She heard him chuckle.

"You didn't find it."

"No. But I do have a couple of photos of promotional bears you might want to look at. They're definitely not the same, but—" she fingered the flyers, lifting them for another cursory glance "—under the circumstances, they may be close enough."

"Well…I'm sort of tied up till later this afternoon."

Disappointment welled in Whitney. What did she expect, she chided herself? That he was going to run right over? A man couldn't sell eight million dollars of real estate a year and not have a few commitments. "I'll just put this information aside for you,'' she said. ''Whenever it's convenient. Or,'' she offered, ''I could drop it in the mail.''

''No, listen, I was thinking about stopping by your place anyway. Amanda's ballet lesson is in forty minutes, and the studio's less than two blocks from your place. You could meet me there and save me some time.''

''You're taking her?'' Disbelief tainted Whitney's reply. ''Why not?''

''But…but…''Whitney glanced at the clock, thinking of all the resort property in the area hungering for a Sold sign from Monroe Realty. ''It's the middle of the afternoon.''

''I know. I intentionally schedule appointments around ballet. It doesn't hurt to close up shop for a couple of hours one afternoon a week. You should try it. Knocking off for a few hours in the middle of the day is good for the soul.''

Would knocking off in the middle of the day to be with Logan, for even a few fleeting minutes, ease this longing in her soul? ''And you want me to try it? To meet you there, and shirk my duties?''

''Absolutely. It's a Thursday. A nice warm day, in the middle of May—'' he rhymed, giving her a moment to consider ''—I say…it's time for all good shopkeepers to come out and play.''

''Cute.'' That old familiar tap dance started playing through her veins.

''C'mon, Whitney. Join us. We didn't have enough time to talk the other night. Meet Amanda. Judge for yourself, and see why this is so important to me. My life is on hold until this is settled.'' The invitation was tempting; it might be one of her few chances to spend time with Logan and get to know his daughter. ''You'll fall in love with her, Whitney,'' he predicted.

She didn't need that. No more falling in love with *anyone* in the Monroe household. ''I don't know,'' she hedged. ''The UPS guy sometimes comes on Thursday.''

She thought she heard him snicker, and immediately felt like a role model for one of the dumb ''blonde'' jokes that were circulating. Maybe it had been a mistake to color her hair.

"You ever been to a ballet class, Whitney?"

"No." Her reply was tinged with a certain amount of regret.

She had wanted to take dance lessons—like Carla Simpson, who had pranced around on her toe shoes during the fourth-grade play—but there had never been enough money when she lived with her mom, and then, later, Gram said spending money on that was just plain foolish. It wasn't like she was going to be a ballerina or anything. As it turned out, she had done something better with her life anyway, because every time she saw a toddler walk away hugging one of her teddies her heart melted.

"It's an experience," he said. "One you'd have to see to appreciate."

"I'd imagine," she said dryly.

"It's only forty-five minutes for the lesson," he wheedled. "But it's about two hours worth of fun."

Whitney gazed indecisively at the Closed sign; it wouldn't take that much to turn it over. She wasn't planning to do anything but stock shelves anyway, and they were a good month away from the tourist season. "I could...probably...meet you there. For a few minutes," she qualified, trying not to sound too eager.

"Terrific. Miss Timlin begins promptly at three-fifteen. If you aren't there in time for stretching and warm-ups, I'll save you a seat."

It was the craziest thing. In her mind's eye she saw him grinning, and it made her feel warm all over.

Chapter Three

Miss Timlin's School of Dance was an institution in Melville. Parents sent their daughters to Miss Timlin's for more than ballet or tap or jazz. They sent them because it was the proper thing to do. Young ladies who went through all twelve years of Miss Timlin's carried themselves with a distinguishable grace. They possessed a presence that made their movements smooth, their voices confident and their smiles benign. It was no surprise to Whitney that Logan chose that for his daughter.

The foyer of Miss Timlin's smelled of old wood and lemon oil. The interior of the great hall was cool, and the mahogany banister curving up to the second-story studio was polished to a satin finish. Whitney looked up, over her head. The antique chandelier, suspended from a tin ceiling, hung from a single tarnished chain. It swayed from the staccatoed thump of little feet on the floor above.

A receptionist greeted Whitney, indicating the session had already started, but that she was welcome to observe, provided she found a seat in the back. *Quietly,* the woman admonished.

Whitney turned to the steps, trying to imagine how Logan felt once a week, as he put his hand to the banister and climbed the magnificent old staircase. She gingerly put her palm across the top of the newel post, then tested the first stair tread. It groaned beneath her weight, like an old woman wearied from raising too many children.

Whitney took the stairs slowly, amazed that Logan had been within blocks of her for months—and yet their paths had never crossed.

At the top, Whitney paused on the landing and peered into the first open doorway. The studio, awash in pink and white leotards, warm-ups and floppy hair bows, teemed with discipline. Miss Timlin, sixty if she was a day, with her gaunt face resembling a road map of wrinkles, and her arms and legs as sinewy as chicken bones, stood sternly at the front of the room. She thumped her staff on the hardwood floor.

"Stretch, Melissa! Hannah! You are not to preen in front of the mirror, you are to reflect upon your position before it." In tights and leotards, Miss Timlin's paunchy middle and sagging breasts were a mere testament to her resilience.

A gaggle of mothers waited, on hard-backed chairs that had been pushed against the wall. Two held magazines, one a book; none of them scanned the copy. Another woman's knitting needles copiously clacked together, but her gaze was riveted to what was happening on the dance floor.

Logan was the only man in the room, and he appeared impervious to be outnumbered by the opposite sex; his attention, too, was directed solely to the activity on the floor.

"Excuse me," Whitney whispered, apologizing to the master knitter as she carefully stepped over a bag of turquoise yarn. She slipped into the chair next to Logan.

His head turned, his eyes rounding into irresistible crescents as he smiled. "Hello," he mouthed. "Glad you could make it."

The chairs were so close that Whitney inadvertently leaned against him as she sat, her shoulder brushing his.

The flesh beneath his dress shirt was hard, warm…and definitely bothersome to her senses. Whitney tried to look unaffected. "I hope Miss Timlin doesn't yell at me for making a disturbance," she whispered, as the aura of his aftershave enveloped them.

"I'll protect you if she does," he whispered, sliding an arm to the back of her chair in order to give her more room.

Whitney's smile was taut, self-conscious. Everyone around them had peeled their eyes off the dance floor, to notice that Logan Monroe had welcomed this newcomer.

Whump, whump. "At the bar, ladies!" Miss Timlin directed, wielding her staff like a shepherdess. "Now, please."

A dozen ballerinas scampered to claim their place at the mirrored wall. Logan nudged Whitney. "That's Amanda," he said. "Second from the left."

The child, with round blue eyes and fat cheeks, exuded a *Shirley Templesque* sparkle. She didn't walk; she pranced. A riot of strawberry-blond curls, bound with a diaphanous pink-and-white scrunchie, and pulled to a curious angle at the top of her head, swung against her nape. She paused long enough to look over her shoulder at her father, then offered up an outrageous wink and an infectious smile.

A chuckle of appreciation rumbled through Logan's chest. Women on either side of them snickered. "She has my comedic sense of timing," he whispered.

"She's darling."

"She's a ham. A darling ham. I know it. And I love it."

Whitney drew a deep, amused breath, and settled back against Logan's arm, to bask in the enthusiasm of a gregarious six-year-old. Another mind-bending matter also weighed heavily on her mind: What brand of cologne did Logan wear?

The lesson ended much too quickly. When it was over, Amanda went flying into Logan's arms.

"Daddy! Did you see it? My plié?"

"I did."

"Much better, don't you think?"

"Without a doubt." He cocked his head, to study her floppy ponytail, then awkwardly tried to pat it back into place. "We still didn't get this hair thing right," he muttered.

Amanda didn't seem to care about that, but her expressive mouth drooped. "I wish Mommy would have been here to see it."

"What?"

"My plié."

"Oh." An uncomfortable moment of silence passed, then Logan pulled her into his arms. "I think, Amanda, that she knows," he said gently. "Mommy loved you so much that she's never really far from you." His forefinger tapped her chest. "She's right here, you know…in your heart."

Amanda nodded bravely, but her eyes were solemn, sad. Whitney's heart wrenched.

"Miss Timlin said I might be a swan in the recital," Amanda announced.

"Really?" Logan pulled back, feigning intrigue.

"If I have another good lesson," she said, dipping her chin as she scooched, uninvited, onto his lap. "That's what she said. The swans get to wear feathers in their hair, you know."

"Ah. Well, either way, feathers or no feathers, I'm proud of you." He gave Amanda a quick, congratulatory hug. "Amanda, there's someone I want you to meet."

Amanda leaned forward. Her gaze, neither friendly nor hostile, unabashedly met Whitney's. "Must be you," she concluded. "You're the only new person here."

"Hi," Whitney said, extending her hand. "I'm Whitney Bloom."

Amanda briefly regarded her, then politely dragged her fingers against Whitney's palm. The greeting was a curious mixture of an infant's patty-cake and an adolescent's high-five. "Like the flower?" she asked.

"Excuse me?" Whitney stopped, perplexed.

"You know. It's a saying. Daddy always says we should bloom where we're planted."

"Oh, he does, does he?" Whitney lifted her eyes, to exchange an amused look with Logan. To her delight, he winked.

"He says it means we have to do our best, no matter where we are or what happens to us."

"I see. Good advice."

"You're lucky to have a name like that," Amanda went on. "Sometime I'm going to get a name I can keep, that's what the social worker says. Of course, I wish I had a name like Daddy's."

Both Logan and Whitney blanched at Amanda's unwitting reference to the muddled adoption.

"Do you have a little girl?" Amanda asked unexpectedly.

The question startled Whitney, and she pulled back, half-afraid of disappointing the child. "No," she said slowly.

"What's the matter? Don't you want to have one?"

"Amanda," Logan reproved. "That's kind of a personal question, even for a chatterbox like you. We don't ask—"

"No, that's okay," Whitney said quickly. "I don't mind. Really." She paused, wondering how much she could safely reveal. "Someday I'd love to have a little girl. More than anything. But I'm not married and, actually, I'd like to have a daddy for my little girl. I'd want to make sure she was safe, and happy, and loved by her mom and dad."

"You don't have a husband?"

An ominous feeling swept over Whitney, making her feel as if she was stepping into something as dangerous as quicksand. "No, not anymore."

Amanda sat back, and thoughtfully regarded Whitney. "My daddy doesn't have my mommy anymore, either."

"I know, and I'm sorry to hear it."

"She went to heaven," Amanda matter-of-factly explained. "Where did your husband go?"

Whitney did a stutter-step over her answer. She certainly couldn't explain to a six-year-old what had led to the breakup of her marriage. For, after Logan caught Kevin skimming money from the petty cash, and threatened to press charges, it had been the last straw for Whitney and her marriage had immediately crumbled. There had never been a blacker, more degrading moment in her life. She suddenly realized how she supported him while he wandered from one job to another, how she'd suffered through his rude behavior and insolence. It had come as an epiphany to her, to realize she had married Kevin for the wrong reasons—and Logan, whether he knew it or not, had had a hand in her decision to move on with her life.

Logan, seeing Whitney's distress, flushed uncomfortably, then leaned over and sternly whispered in his daughter's ear.

Suddenly a wry response struck Whitney, and she impulsively offered it up. "My husband," she announced glibly, "went to California. With a cardboard suitcase, and a beat-up Chevrolet. And, let me tell you, he was a funny sight, going down the highway."

Logan clamped his lips over an irrepressible smile, his eyes shuttering closed. Amanda's lips wiggled, even as she looked genuinely confused.

When it hit Whitney, she was appalled at the jingle she'd just concocted. "I'm sorry," she apologized. "I didn't explain that very well. And I didn't mean—" lowering her voice, she caught Logan's eye "—to make it sound like…"

"It's okay," he mouthed over Amanda's head. Then, he chuckled. "Whitney and I went to school together, Amanda, and for as long as I've known her, she has always put an interesting spin on life."

Nagging embarrassment colored her cheeks, but Whitney took the plunge, determined to be honest with Amanda— and with Logan. "Amanda," she said seriously, "my ex-husband wasn't very happy—and he wanted things I didn't want. So, how it ended up was that he left—and I stayed.

We got a divorce because we couldn't be happy together
and agree on how to live our life."

"Is he ever coming back?"

Whitney shook her head, afraid to look at Logan, afraid
of what she'd see in his eyes. "No. Never."

Amanda's gaze never wavered. "Then you're all alone,
too. Like us."

The candid observation knocked the wind out of Whitney. She steeled herself to show no emotion. "Single, and
independent," she confided, leaning closer to Amanda.
"It's not a bad thing for a woman to be. Honest."

Amanda studied her, quizzically. Then she reached over
and carefully touched the gold charm, the teddy bear that
Whitney always wore. "I like that," she said shyly.

"You do?" Whitney's smile reached her eyes. "You
know there's a story behind that little bear."

"There is?" Amanda's eyes widened hopefully.

"Mmm-hmm. When I was a little girl, not much bigger
than you, we had to move. We were kind of in a hurry, so
my mom thought she'd leave some of our stuff and go back
and get it later. But there was this mix-up, and everything
got lost. All my books, my dolls, all my favorite things.
They were all gone. Not one thing was left."

Amanda's face fell. "You must have felt awful," she
said soberly, dropping the charm, to awkwardly pat the
back of Whitney's hand.

"For a while I did. But then my gram, who had some
old scraps of fabric, helped me make a rag doll. It turned
out so wonderful that we started thinking we could make
a teddy bear." For emphasis, Whitney rolled her eyes.
"Well, we had the craziest looking teddy bear you ever did
see. My gram said it looked like something the cat dragged
in."

Amanda laughed, imagining.

"So my gram went out and bought me a brand-new
teddy bear, and I thought it was the best present ever."
Whitney glanced up at Logan, but his eyes were brooding,

dark. "I..." Whitney hesitated, "I have a little store not far from here, and everything in it has teddy bears on it."

"Really?"

"Really."

Amanda sat back, in the circle of Logan's arms, considering. "Daddy?"

"Yes?"

"Is that where you got the coloring books and stuff?"

"As a matter of fact, yes, at Whitney's shop."

"Maybe sometime, Amanda, you'd like to visit me there, and see all the teddy bear things."

"Can we, Daddy? Do you think we can go?"

"What I think, gumdrop," Logan said, carefully avoiding an answer, "is that you've pestered Whitney long enough. Come on. You ready for our weekly pilgrimage?"

"Can Whitney come? Please? This could be the day for the Lollapalooza."

Logan pulled back, baffled. This was a first. Since Jill's death, Amanda had been reluctant to invite people into her life. She didn't warm up to people anymore, not as quickly as she used to. But, with Whitney, he saw vestiges of the old Amanda coming back.

"That's a great idea, to invite Whitney," he agreed. "Well?" he slid Whitney a sideways glance, and didn't bother to explain. Everyone in Melville knew the Lollapalooza was the Ice Crème Shoppe's 27 scoop, thirteen topping treat. "What do you say? Can you join us?"

"Oh...no, I'd feel like I was intruding..." If Whitney could have kicked herself all the way home, she would have. She'd automatically offered up the no, and passed up another rare opportunity to be with Logan.

"Whitney. C'mon. Join us," he insisted. "The Lollapalooza may be a little too much, but maybe another time...for a special occasion..." He lifted one shoulder higher than the other, letting the suggestion hang.

"You're goading me into playing hooky," Whitney chided. "I have rent to pay and shelves to stock."

"And you work too hard. You're too dedicated." He glanced at his watch. "It's almost closing time anyway. A four o'clock sundae is the perfect way to end the day and spoil your supper."

Whitney considered supper. It would be another single serving size eaten in front of the TV.

"My treat," Logan persuaded as Amanda slipped off his lap.

"They have Chocoholics Anonymous," Amanda said, balancing on one foot as she wiggled the other bare one into a sandal. "When I don't get that, I get Mississippi Sludge."

Whitney raised an eyebrow, and squelched a smile over Amanda's Mithithippi Thludge lisp. "Mmm. Sounds yummy."

"Daddy says I'm a chocolate freak."

"A trait I share," Whitney admitted. "I never ever pass up chocolate."

Logan offered Amanda an oversize shirt to slip over her tights and leotards. The shirt, though clean, looked like it had spent the last few weeks forgotten in the bottom of the dryer. "I take it that's a yes," Logan said, as he helped Amanda turn the sleeve right side out.

"Okay. I can't refuse. Besides, the day's shot anyway."

Logan's expression grew pensive, thoughtful. Then he looked at her, and winked. "Somehow, I get the impression it's just beginning."

The Ice Crème Shoppe was rocking. A group of teen-agers were celebrating a sixteenth birthday and the jukebox was cranked up full-blast. Amanda, who knew two of the teens as baby-sitters, didn't miss a trick. She was elbow to elbow with them, *oohing* and *aahing* as the guest of honor opened her presents.

Seeing she was occupied, Whitney extracted the flyers on the teddy bears and offered them to Logan. They were in a circular back booth, isolated and protected from the noisy crowd. "Here. Look at these. See what you think."

He studied the hot pink flyers, then stopped at the full page advertisement she'd torn from a collector's catalog.

Fascinated by Logan's intensity, Whitney couldn't imagine ever tiring of his focus, his concentration. He'd always been like that. In high school chemistry, Logan could crack jokes one minute, then buckle down and become absorbed in the most complicated lab experiment the next. That part of him had always intrigued her.

"Whitney. I don't think...this is quite what... They aren't right." He shook his head. "How close are they?"

"Not very."

A sinking feeling washed over Whitney. She'd spent three grueling days hunting for this teddy bear, and she knew, from what Logan said, time was short. "Logan," she said carefully, "this could take a while."

He folded up the papers and reluctantly handed them back to her. "I never imagined the world had gone teddy bear crazy. I thought I'd just get another one...for old time's sake—or a fresh start. For her, you know." He shrugged, trying to make it look like it didn't matter. His gaze narrowed, the blue color almost disappearing as he looked over to Amanda, who, at the player piano, sang along with the crowd.

Whitney watched Amanda from the corner of her eye. "Logan, why don't you bring her over to my shop and let her look at the teddy bears? Maybe she'll find something she likes. We could do it later tonight, or..." She let the words trail off, lifting her shoulders.

Logan tapped his thumb against the table's edge, momentarily debating. "I can't tonight. I've got a seven o'clock appointment for a closing."

Whitney chose to ignore his abrupt tone. "Maybe another time?"

A shadow crossed his handsome features. "Maybe."

Whitney knew it would never happen. Not knowing what

to say, she feigned interest in all the activity around her, swiping at the perspiration on her water glass.

Logan sighed. "You have to understand, Whit, that I'm being selfish about this. I don't want her to just pick out another toy...it means more to me than that."

"I understand."

The strains of *"Happy Birthday to you,"* faded, then someone tacked on a falsetto version of *"and we do...ooo mean you."*

"This is stupid. How the hell can you replace something like that?"

Logan's angry words sent chills through Whitney; she knew he wasn't talking about the teddy bear; he was talking about Amanda. When she was six, Whitney would have crawled over hot coals and bargained with the devil to have a daddy like that.

"You can't, Logan," she said softly. "You can't replace this wonderful, precious child you've raised. But...if it helps...I'll find you the bear. I promise."

"Thanks. I..." Logan's attention remained on the partygoers clustered around the piano. Then, with a burst of energy that startled Whitney, he swiveled on the bench beside her, and tossed an arm around her shoulders.

Whitney went weak, feeling too much of him: the warmth, the bone and sinew. She shivered, her mind fast-forwarding to recount how many times he'd thrown an arm around her in high school. Three? Four? She'd cherished every moment of his attention, and every time he made her feel special, she had fallen a little bit more in love with him.

"I don't want you to think I don't appreciate all you're doing," he said, leaning closer and making the words go fuzzy against her ear. "I do."

Whitney's eyes involuntarily closed, and she savored the inexplicable whisper of sexual attraction. "You baffle me," she said without thinking.

"What?" He absently rolled his thumb over the shoulder seam of her sweater. "Why?" he probed.

Whitney opened her eyes, aware Logan's face was only inches from hers. "Because you have it all, Logan. You own a successful company, you have a lovely home, and a standing in the community. Friends. Family. And yet your priority seems to be keeping your little family together."

His thumb stopped stroking the ridge of her shoulder seam. "Why should that surprise you?"

"Because this is your opportunity to walk away without any responsibility."

"You think I'm the kind of man who would do that?"

"Most men would. I've known men who've walked away for a whole lot less." He stared at her, the pressure on her shoulder going heavy.

"That's what doesn't make sense to me. Because you could—and you don't."

"Then you've known the wrong kind of men, Whitney. I guess you've known men who wanted the easy way out."

Whitney grimaced, thinking Logan's appraisal of her ex-husband must be somewhere between a cad and a cheat. What must he think of her for picking him?

"I've never been a man who took—or even wanted—the easy way out." Logan studied her guarded reaction, and realized he'd delved a little too deeply. Her mouth wobbled—just enough to make the words kissable and comforting simultaneously roll through his head. Her eyes had a spark of fear, of vulnerability; one he wanted to douse and soothe. "Whitney?" he asked.

She nodded, but wouldn't look at him. "Hey. I could have used you as a role model," she said tremulously. "You know, the first man in my life, my dad, wasn't ever around. Not ever. I remember my mom used to joke, and refer to him as the 'phantom,' the guy who simply visited in the middle of the night." She hesitated. "And I guess I don't have to tell you about my ex. He was a piece of work, wasn't he?"

Empathy washed through Logan, and he shook his head, imagining the kind of verbal abuse she'd endured. "Whitney," he said finally, "I know the men in your life left a lasting impression, but…" His hand strayed to her temple, to push back a wispy strand of her summer-blond hair and hook it behind her ear. "I'd like to leave one, too. Just a different one."

"Logan—"

"No, listen. You've gone out of your way for me over this bear thing. If you need something, ever, you can always count on me. Okay?" he asked gently, his fingertips drifting down the smooth column of her neck before loosely settling on her shoulders. He leaned toward her, and without waiting for an answer, he impulsively brushed his lips against Whitney's temple.

Against the side of his mouth he felt her eyelashes flutter, and they left tingly butterfly kisses in their wake. Her skin was so soft, and her hair smelled like strawberry shampoo. His lips inched down and he found himself spiraling into a vortex of male need as his mouth hovered near hers.

Yet the moment he felt her tremble, he pulled away.

Her eyes were huge and round, and filled with surprise and trepidation. "That," she said, her voice jumping off track, "is a count-on-me kiss?"

For a moment Logan was so appalled at what he'd just done—in the middle of the Ice Crème Shoppe, no less— he couldn't answer. What had gotten into him? Being *that* familiar with Whitney Bloom? "No, it's a—" he swallowed "—a thank-you."

Whitney's jaw jutted slightly forward, as if she was hurt, and the silvery-white scar quivered as she lifted her chin. The brilliant color of her dark eyes faded between narrowed lids. "I don't need that kind of a thank-you, Logan," she said. "Two words will do it."

Chapter Four

Logan lived on the other side of "the point," in a small cluster of homes that nestled into irregular chunks of land around Lake Justice. The moment her tires bumped over his easement, Whitney's pulse quickened and her breathing grew erratic. What was she doing here in this section of Melville, walking into his life as if she belonged?

She forced herself to pull up next to the three and a half stall garage and climbed out of the car, squinting against the sunshine.

"Hey, Whitney! Down here!"

Whitney spun on her heel. Two hundred feet away, Logan, bare-chested and up to his knees in water, stood next to the dock. A white sand beach, gouged with clogs, and sand pails and lounge chairs, crooked around the uneven shoreline. Moored farther out was a sleek speedboat, a lazy looking pontoon and two jet skis. She waved, an involuntary smile sliding onto her lips.

He lifted a bare arm, and beckoned. "Come on down!"

Her stomach clenched, and her blood ran warm, then hot, as that old familiar tap dance drummed through her veins.

Against the glassy water, he was all angles and chiseled planes. The neat wedge of his shoulders. A chunk of sculpted chest over his tapered waist. Lanky arms. Solid legs.

Whitney shivered, staring down at Logan Monroe's near nakedness. He was at least six inches taller than she. How in the heck was she going to come eyeball to chest hair with him and know where to look? Right now her eyes were practically falling out of their sockets.

The hems of his swim trunks were wet, the weight pulling the fabric down from his belly, to expose a pencil-thin patch of white skin. The rest of him—his shoulders, his chest—were nothing but lean, mean bronze.

She started moving down the path to his private beach, crazily thinking that her body worked as if on autopilot: her senses honed in like radar, her ears pitched to the gently lapping water, her sights were set on Logan as if he were a target. A whispery soft sensation struck her, near the temple, where Logan had kissed her barely a week ago.

She had to get her reactions under control soon. Logan Monroe was big trouble, she reminded herself.

Trouble with a capital *T*.

T as in tall, tanned and teeming with testosterone.

It wasn't her fault, to be thinking like this. There ought to be a law. Men like Logan Monroe should not be permitted to stand around half-naked in Lake Justice. It messed up the female brain wave pattern.

Oh, God have mercy on her aching soul. She shouldn't have come here. It was just like a couple of weeks ago, when he came in the store and intuition told her something was going to happen. Today, she was going to make a fool of herself, she knew it.

She stepped onto the beach, and fine white sand trickled through the straps of her sandals. Down here, two hundred feet from the house, the air stirred up a virtual potpourri of smells. Honeysuckle and sun-baked wood. Fish and suntan lotion. Gas and motor oil. Ripples of water thudded dully against the fiberglass boat. The pontoon bounced awkwardly over them, the aluminum offering up hollow burps of noise.

"Well, hello," Logan greeted, water lapping at his ankles. "This is a nice surprise."

Whitney smiled, and lifted her hand to shield her eyes from the glare off the water.

"I suppose you wanted to see if I'm doing a good job, repairing this dock."

"No," she countered, her protected gaze drifting over his body. "I wanted to come down and see you this bare—" She choked and immediately coughed, momentarily slapping her knuckles against her mouth. "I mean, come down and show you this *teddy* bear."

Logan raised an eyebrow.

"It, um—"

Logan sauntered nearer. Water droplets glistened like a lure on his shoulders, his chest.

"You're bare. I mean...your teddy bear." She let the explanation dissolve. "You know," she said, going breathless, "maybe I caught you at a bad time...."

Logan chuckled, and grabbed a T-shirt that was hanging over a post at the end of the dock. "No. Not at all." He stretched the hem of his shirt between his fists, then plunged his arms into the sleeves, accordian pleating it to his elbows.

"I stopped by your office and your secretary said I could find you here, that it wouldn't be a problem. But—"

"It isn't." He lifted his arms to pull the shirt over his head.

"I feel like I'm intruding. You probably have a lot of work to do."

His shoulders slumped, and both elbows dropped as he paused. He still hadn't pulled it on, and the T-shirt sagged against his middle as he frowned at her. "Whitney. You're a friend. You're doing me a huge favor. You're making it sound like I wouldn't take time for you." He cocked his head. "By the way, aren't you taking off in the middle of a workweek? Isn't that against your nature, or something?"

She shrugged. "Sort of. But I have someone who helps me out on Tuesdays. It's my day to run errands, go to the bank and the post office, that kind of thing. But today was slow, and it was so nice out, I just thought I'd make this an errand and drop it off."

"Really?"

"Mmm."

"Great. Since you've got the time, then, I've got an errand for you." He intentionally paused, then winked. "Meet me in the middle of Lake Justice."

Whitney stared at him, confused.

"Amanda's got a half day of school, and she's up at the house, getting us lemonade. The sandwiches and chips are already stowed. We were just about to have a lazy afternoon and take the pontoon out. Kick off those sandals and hop on board."

"Oh, I—" Whitney quickly fumbled in the pocket of her slacks, to pull out the copy of the teddy she wanted him to see. She couldn't spend any time with Logan. She couldn't. He'd already upended her hormones, and made her give in to wishful thinking. Paper in hand, she tried to smooth out the creases before extending it.

"Show me later," Logan advised smoothly, glancing up to the back of the house. "We already have company."

Whitney swiveled and looked over her shoulder. Amanda trotted down the path, her blond hair flying, and a jug of lemonade banging against her knees. "Hi, Whitney!" she hollered. "I didn't know you were coming!"

Whitney stuffed the copy back into her pocket, opening her mouth to object.

Behind her, and over her shoulder, Logan warned, "Don't. She'll be disappointed."

When she turned back, Logan was yanking the shirt over his head. He pulled the Canton Beach Club shirt down, straightening the hem as he grinned. "I'm pretty good at surprises, aren't I, pip?"

"The best," Amanda agreed breathlessly, running up to them, and setting the jug at a haphazard angle on her toes. She took in Whitney's shell-pink slacks, and matching sleeveless top. "Didn't you bring your suit?" An edge of disappointment tainted her question.

"I...well, no...."

"Whitney made the mistake of thinking when I said we'd take the pontoon out, we'd stay in it." He rolled his eyes at Amanda. "We have to educate her about the ways of the water. We'll have to convince her how much fun it is to jump off and splash around a little."

"Oh." Sympathy washed over Amanda, and she grew solemn. "You aren't afraid of the water, are you?"

"Actually, my swimming strokes are a little rusty," she admitted.

"Daddy can help you," she said. "I used to be afraid of the water, but he taught me how to swim. He used to let me put my arms around his neck, and then hold me, so I wouldn't drown."

Whitney imagined her arms around Logan's neck, as the heat of their near-naked bodies entwined in the cool waters of Lake Justice. Drown? Criminey, she was already drowning in a waterworld of fantasy.

She dared to look up, only to find Logan's gaze riveted to her response. Whitney flushed.

"So, I just put my arms around his neck—" she said, trying to make light of the moment.

"And he'll never let anything bad happen to you," Amanda said.

"You're sure of that?" she murmured.

"I know he won't. Because he's the best."

The child's confirmation gripped her heart.

"Looks like we're just gonna have to convince her, pip."

Amanda nodded, picking the jug up off her toes, then

grimacing as she flexed her big toe. "You'll bring your suit next time, won't you?"

"Sure. Next time." Whitney knew she was extending a false promise, but she couldn't bear to hurt Amanda right now.

Peanut butter and jelly sandwiches had never tasted so good. They both knew it was time to head in, so Logan reluctantly steered the pontoon toward the dock while Whitney debated about the last unwrapped sandwich.

"Polish it off," he encouraged.

"I don't know what's the matter with me," she apologized, feeling like a glutton, "I'm so hungry."

"Being on the water works up an appetite."

His observation was all the encouragement she needed. Whitney caved in, and pulled apart the plastic wrap. She broke the sandwich in half and offered the other half to Logan.

The gesture, insignificant as it seemed, appeared to startle him. He paused for a moment, staring at the extended sandwich.

"What?" she asked. "You don't want it?"

"No, I...it's just a reminder. That's all."

Whitney frowned, guessing he'd made a mental note to pick up another loaf of bread. She turned both halves over, to see if the bread was moldy.

Logan snorted. "No. The sandwich is fine. It's just... well, Jill used to break pieces off, too, and feed me when we were driving, or on the water like this. Seeing you do it, like that...made me think..."

Discomfort washed over Whitney. "I understand," she said quietly.

But she didn't understand, not at all. As much as she empathized with Logan's loss, she didn't want to be someone to remind him of—or even compare against—his late wife.

"Thanks." He put his hand out, palm side up for the sandwich.

Logan's recollection had taken the edge off of her appetite, so, without saying anything more, she offered him the larger half.

Amanda drowsily sprawled in the back of the boat, unconcerned with their conversation as she stared up at the marshmallow white clouds overhead. She was on her back, on her Pokémon towel, with one ankle crossed over her bent knee. Occasionally she hummed an off-key version of "Popeye, the Sailor Man." Earlier, when Whitney had unexpectedly harmonized in, offering her best tugboat imitation of "toot, toot," Amanda had howled and begged for her to do it over and over again. The three of them had improvised, then dissolved into laughter. It had been an unforgettable afternoon. Amanda was a peach, and Logan was every bit the doting father. Whitney felt lucky just to be with them.

"That's the best part of marriage, you know," Logan went on, oblivious to her thoughts, as he took a huge chunk of the sandwich. "The little things. Sharing a soda. Drinking out of the same glass. Letting someone dab a napkin against your mouth and brush away the crumbs. Or stop you while you're walking, and push the tags on your clothes back on the inside, where they belong."

Hearing the yearning in his voice, Whitney grew increasingly uneasy. She tried to laugh. "You're making it sound more like you need a caretaker."

"Maybe I do." He tilted the sandwich at her. "It's not such a bad thing, Whitney, to look out for someone else. To put them first in your life. To have someone do the same for you."

"Logan?"

"Hmm?" The right side of his cheek was swollen, as he thoughtfully swiped, with his tongue, at the peanut butter.

"I was joking. About the caretaker thing."

"I know." He swallowed and nodded, concentrating on

avoiding the wake of two jet skis. "You probably don't want me to go all serious on you."

"It's not that, exactly." The pontoon rocked, tilting crazily over the waves. She clutched the armrest, knowing the conversation was headed into potentially dangerous waters.

"I just have these memories," he said, his hands tightening on the steering wheel. "Sometimes when I least expect them." He turned the wheel slightly, aligning the boat toward the dock in the distance and carefully taking them out of the wake. "Having you offer me that sandwich reminded me of Jill."

"Logan—"

"I know. You don't want to hear about Jill. People never know what to say. Talking about her makes them uncomfortable."

Whitney ran her thumbnail along the vinyl piping of the mate's chair. She wished he wasn't wearing his sunglasses. She wanted to see his eyes, to gauge the emotion that was still holding him captive to a bunch of memories. "I just wonder if you really want to tell me those things. If, maybe, they're too intimate and personal. Maybe you'll regret talking about them—especially with me."

"What? Why?"

The last of the sandwich stuck in her throat. She shook her head, still unable to look at him. "I don't know. I—"

"How, Whitney, could you possibly make this hurt any worse?" his voice lifted incredulously. "If anything you've only helped heal it. For me, and Amanda."

"I haven't done anything," she denied.

"You're helping me find something that's pretty important," he said, alluding to the teddy bear. She had shown the crumpled photo to him earlier, and he had shaken his head, indicating that wasn't the bear he was looking for. "And Amanda genuinely likes you." he said. "I haven't seen her warm up to someone like that in months."

A glimmer of gratification rose in Whitney.

"You're a friend, Whitney. You've listened to me, and

taken all my fears about losing Amanda to heart.'' With the dock fifty yards away, he pulled back on the throttle. ''Nobody else understands, not like you.''

Whitney went weak all over. His praise and kind words only made her more vulnerable. ''You know,'' she said shakily, ''we're muddling up this teddy bear transaction with ice cream and boat rides and peanut butter sandwiches. You put a few nice words in the mix and it could be all over.''

He chuckled, and cut the engine. The front of the pontoon bumped against the dock.

Amanda stirred, yawning as she pulled herself into a sitting position. ''Look—'' she pointed, squinting up the path and to the back of the house ''—we've got more company.''

Both Whitney and Logan glanced up, where a woman, clad in a dark blue business suit, waited. She switched the briefcase to her other hand, and waved.

Logan swore under his breath. ''Terrific. One bad ending to one great day,'' he muttered fiercely, ripping his sunglasses off and tossing them onto the dash.

Amanda used the last of her energy to race up the incline, dragging her towel behind her. ''Hi, Madeline!'' she called. ''I had a half day of school.''

Logan and Whitney climbed steadily after her. After his burst of temper, Logan had reined in his emotions and grown quiet. He hadn't offered any explanations and he knew Whitney would be too reluctant to ask. He was grateful for that.

''My. That sounds like fun.''

Whitney stopped short, making Logan stumble against her. He caught her before they could both tumble to the ground. Her surprise was clearly visible and she turned in the circle of his arms. Once again, even in his despair, Logan was struck by how soft, how willowy Whitney was.

''Madeline Enright's your caseworker?''

"You know her?" His palms gently slipped down to her elbows, steadying her.

"For years and years, I've donated all my teddy bears from my trade-in days to social services. She picked up another batch a couple of months ago."

"Good," Logan said, pausing long enough to push a wispy strand of hair off her cheek. "That means you've got some pull with the woman. Put in a good word for me, will you?"

Whitney grinned. "What? A testament to your character?"

He lifted a noncommittal shoulder. "I don't know. If that's what it takes. Every time I see her, I figure she's going to say the jig's up and the adoption's over."

"It's that serious?"

"It seems to be, yes."

"You think, today, without any notice at all...?"

"Whitney, I honestly don't know where this is going. Not from day to day." The confirmation seemed troubling to Whitney, and for a split second, Logan regretted taking her into his confidence. He knew that she'd been bounced around a lot as a kid, so this was probably bringing back a lot of bad memories. "Don't worry about it. She drops in and we visit, that's all. She just checks to see how things are going."

"And they aren't going well, are they?"

He looked down at her lovely face, and felt the most incredible urge to protect her. Even from his own troubles. "They're going as well as I can possibly make them."

Whitney pulled back, and together, they climbed the path. Amanda and Madeline, deep in conversation, were discussing the finer points of wearing a life jacket.

"I can swim really good now, but Daddy says I always have to wear my jacket. It's for safety, he says. Just so nothing happens to me."

"Mmm, we wouldn't want that." Madeline, who was in her mid-forties, had brackets of smile lines in her peaches-

and-cream complexion, both at the corners of her eyes and her mouth. She had perceptive blue eyes, and hair that was just beginning to gray. "Why, Whitney," she exclaimed, "what are you doing here?"

"Oh, we're—"

"Old friends," Logan put in, sliding the heel of his hand against her shoulder blade, letting his fingers curl over her shoulder.

"Really?" Madeline looked from one to the other, as if she were trying to measure the depth of their friendship.

"It was such a great day, I coaxed Whitney into a ride on the pontoon."

"Wonderful." She looked curiously at Whitney's long pants, her sandals. Logan wore swimming trunks, a T-shirt and canvas tennis shoes without socks.

"Oh, I just came from work," Whitney explained, lifting the toes of her sandals. "It was sort of a spontaneous thing."

"Next time she's bringing her suit," Amanda announced. "And Daddy's going to teach her how to swim."

Madeline arched a thinly penciled brow. "Really?"

"Those are the plans," Logan confirmed.

Whitney smiled noncommittally.

Madeline turned back to her charge. "Well, you're looking good," she said to Amanda. "I think you've grown another inch."

"I've outgrown almost all my school clothes. But school's almost out," she confided, "so it doesn't really matter. We're cutting off all my pants and making them into shorts. I'm going to wear those when Daddy and I go to the zoo this summer. And—guess what? He's making me a playhouse!"

"Oh?" Madeline's enthusiasm waned, and her expression grew guarded.

"I've wanted one forever. There's going to be a front porch and everything."

"Amanda?" Logan interjected. "Why don't you go up and change? But hop in the shower first."

"Okay. Bye." Amanda immediately excused herself, without argument.

"She's tired," Logan said after Amanda had closed the patio door behind her. "She fell asleep in the boat on the way back."

"Well," Whitney began, "it's been a great afternoon, I should probably be—"

"No. Stay," Logan interrupted. "You know Madeline. You know why she's here. No secret about that. Come on," he invited, "let's sit out on the patio. There's plenty of chairs and we can sit down and talk."

Whitney debated. She knew she should leave and let Logan talk candidly with Madeline. But he obviously wanted her to stick around, and she felt an incredible loyalty to help him out. She knew how much he wanted to keep Amanda. If, like he said, she could put in one good word for him...just one...

"Logan," Madeline said, when they were all seated. "I hate to bring this up, but Amanda mentioned you lost another housekeeper."

"Last week," he confirmed.

"How many is that now?"

"Three."

"That many?"

His smile was grim. "I call it the 'went-back' syndrome. One went back to school, one went back to her husband, and one went back to California to care for her grandchildren."

Madeline nodded, but she didn't offer up one smidgen of empathy. "I see. Then...I guess you don't mind if I speak freely?" she asked, indicating she needed to talk, even in Whitney's presence.

"No, not at all."

"The agency is concerned Amanda may need more consistency."

"She's got me," he joked. "How much more consistent can you get?"

"It took you a long time to find the last housekeeper, didn't it?"

"Madeline. You aren't going to fault me for being particular, are you?" He tried to keep the light banter up, but knew it wasn't getting him anywhere. Even Whitney looked uncomfortable. Both hands were in her lap, and she worried the knuckles of her left hand between forefinger and thumb.

"I'm *glad* you're so particular," Madeline finally said. "There's never been a question that Amanda's been safe. I have to say, too, that she seemed happier today than I've seen her in a long, long time. But I've got to tell you, Logan, I've been worried by her withdrawal, especially since she was always such an outgoing child."

"Well, we had a great time out on the pontoon today," he said, his cheeks hurting from making his smile as wide as possible. "Summer's coming on. There's lots to do, lots to look forward to. I want to get to that playhouse right away, and—"

"And lots of additional responsibility for you, too, isn't there?" Madeline asked.

"I consider it temporary. Amanda's in the after-school program right now, and I'm cutting back on work—"

"Again?"

He didn't reply.

"Logan. You're juggling housekeepers, baby-sitters, day care programs. There are people in and out of the house all the time, strangers to adjust and adapt to, this constant turnover, and chaos..."

Logan shot Whitney a glance. Her head was bent, her mouth in a taut line as she trained her eyes on the tips of her sandals. Dammit. If she'd just help him out here, endorse his character, sanction his intentions. Do anything. Something. Paint him up and make him look like a saint.

Witness his clumsy attempts to do the right thing. Testify that he was sincere, honest, and committed.

Lie, if she had to.

Couldn't Whitney see the old bat was setting him up, drawing the noose tighter, preparing to snatch Amanda from his very arms?

"Logan, I recently had a second interview with a lovely couple who could provide a solid, stable environment for Amanda. I only want you to consider it." Madeline's voice had firmed, going no-nonsense. "I know you've tried. But I'm coming to the conclusion it would be in the best interest of the child. Because, without a mother, I'm afraid—"

Whitney's head shot up. "But Amanda's going to have a mother," she blurted.

"Excuse me?" Madeline stopped, confused.

"Me," she said, a bit breathlessly. "Amanda likes me— and that's good because—" in mere anticipation of what she was going to say, Logan felt his eyes widen, and his jaw slide off center "—we're getting married."

Chapter Five

"**Y**ou're getting—" Madeline drew the words out as if she was measuring and framing them with an exacto knife "—married?"

As startled as he was, Logan tried not to gulp like a glass-eyed guppy. He stiffly nodded, and vaguely noticed a guilty flush crawl up Whitney's neck.

"This is kind of...sudden. Isn't it?"

Logan took a ragged breath and tried like hell to smile over it. Okay. He'd play along. For now. "We've known each other for years."

"Really?" Madeline looked to Whitney for confirmation. "That long?"

"Since study hall, tenth grade," Whitney put in, her voice two notches higher than usual, and quavering like a scratched record. In her lap, her hands remained clenched, her knuckles white.

Logan blanched, and pity washed over him; Whitney never could lie worth a damn. He automatically did the most responsible thing he could think of to rescue her. He reached over for Whitney's hand, snared it from her lap and gave it a light, affectionate squeeze. "She's nervous," he said. "We haven't told anyone yet."

Madeline lifted both brows, her eyes pinpoints of light. "Not even Amanda?"

"We didn't think—"

"We wanted—"

Both Whitney and Logan grew quiet, darting furtive glances at each other.

"We haven't told her yet," Whitney emphasized.

"Because we wanted to give her more time," Logan added. "So she could get to know Whitney better. Adjust and all that."

"Well, I have to say, you've really caught me off guard here. I didn't realize you were dating again, Logan. Much less in a serious relationship." Madeline pushed her briefcase aside, as if she were piqued. Then she leaned forward. "But it does appear Amanda is delighted to be with Whitney. She told me you were singing with her on the boat."

Whitney smiled weakly, her expression tremulous. "Yes, I guess our brains got a little—" she shot Logan an apprehensive glance "—waterlogged singing songs. 'My Bonnie.' 'Row, Row, Row Your Boat.' We just sang anything that popped into our heads."

"She said something about Popeye."

"Yes, she likes my toot-toot."

Logan took the plunge, playing the facade of the smitten fiancé to the hilt. "So do I," he said affectionately. "I love your little toot-toot."

Whitney flustered to a deeper shade of red. Somehow, seeing her like that, made the situation a whole lot more endearing and a little bit more tolerable.

Offering up a sympathetic "boys will be boys" smile, Madeline deftly changed the subject. "Still…about the wedding. Logan. Whitney. Tell me you're doing this for the right reasons."

A thousand warnings torpedoed through Logan's mind.

It was too soon. It was too complicated. It was too damn crazy.

He cleared his throat, and wished like hell he could clear his mind. Everything was all upside down, and topsy-turvy. He was attracted to Whitney...but marry her? On a whim? In the hopes of hanging on to Amanda, and salvaging the adoption? How could he use her this way? In the forefront of what little gray matter he had left, ethics and duplicity were dueling it out.

Still, he may as well keep making the right noises—at least until he knew where they were going with this thing.

"I know it seems..." He groped for the right word, knowing it was an *s* word. Selfish, sexy and sinful surfaced like hot points in his brain. He made a show of stroking Whitney's fingertips, his thumb sliding over her ovaled nails. Then it struck him. "Sudden. Yeah. I know this seems sudden."

Madeline tilted her head, her brow furrowing, as if he'd just taken two steps back in the conversation. "Yes," she said. "I think I mentioned that."

It was as sudden as the devil's drop into hell, he wanted to reply.

"But we've talked," Whitney interjected, "about Jill, and Amanda. And how I fit into what it takes to heal."

A prickle inched over Logan's scalp. Whitney had succinctly paraphrased everything he'd said before they'd docked the pontoon. His revelation had affected her, and for some strange reason that mattered. It dearly mattered. She'd listened, and remembered what he'd said.

He continued to stroke her fingers, vaguely wondering what prompted her to offer that up. He'd never heard her utter Jill's name before. Not even when they'd spoken of his grief, or his marriage.

"Well. My. This sort of changes things. I mean, I don't have to be told how much Whitney cares about children. I've known that for years. And she's kind, and good-hearted." Madeline suddenly pulled her gaze from their joined hands, and gave a dazzling smile, her eyelashes fluttering. "Whitney, I can't believe you didn't mention this."

Whitney lifted both shoulders, her features crumpling apologetically. "Actually, I—I didn't know myself."

"Oh?"

An awkward second slipped away. "The last time I saw you, I mean."

"Things just happened," Logan added. "Quickly. Rather quickly."

Whitney leaned a shoulder into him, her elbow narrowly missing his rib cage.

"We weren't going to tell anyone because—"

"You don't have to explain again, Whitney. I understand." Madeline waggled her hand between them. "You're both bright, intelligent people. I'm convinced you'd want to do the right thing. Especially for Amanda. But," she cautioned, "let's wait and see how she takes the news. Children have a way of…rejecting stepmothers. Especially those who try to fill in. You have to be aware of that."

Whitney's hand, still in his, immediately shook.

"Logan," Madeline went on, "let me drop the professionalism for a minute. Off the record, okay?" Logan steeled himself, and sandwiched Whitney's trembling hand between his. He was half-afraid Madeline had seen through the ruse and intended to accuse them of fraud and deceit. For an instant, he visualized a confrontation, and Amanda being taken kicking and screaming from his house. He couldn't breathe, and everything started turning black. "I see no reason why, if you get married right away, and everything goes as you hope it will, that the adoption couldn't be finalized."

Logan stared at her, stunned. His grasp on Whitney loosened. Air started surging into his lungs. Beside him, Whitney sagged, flabbergasted.

"Don't be so surprised," Madeline chided. "I know that's what you both want."

For a moment, there was only the sound of the wind in the trees, of the water lapping against the shore, of a bumblebee hovering over the deck rail.

"We do," they said in unison.

Madeline chuckled. "You can say that part later. Until then, if Whitney has no objections, I'll go ahead and do her background check. It's a formality. This becomes a gray area, you see, as the home is already licensed. Of course, Logan's been Amanda's foster dad for three years and was already in the middle of the adoption proceedings, so things could go rather quickly. Whitney? The background check…?"

"No problem," she said, her voice barely above a whisper. "Whatever you need."

Madeline leaned back, her eyes narrowed, as if judging their fate. "Well, Logan, it looks like you may have won this round. Whitney, my best wishes. I guess I don't have to tell you what kind of a guy Logan is—but I do hope you realize what kind of situation you're getting into."

Logan endured Whitney's sideways glance. He didn't dare return the look; his heart was beating too wildly.

Then, with the mind-boggling thought of Whitney in his bed and in his house, Logan blindly accepted what he presumed were Madeline's congratulations.

Logan and Whitney stood in the driveway of his palatial home, his arm tucked neatly around her waist as they watched Madeline pull out onto the highway. Behind them, a motorboat *chirred* through the water, above them the splatter of Amanda's shower could be heard through the open window. They stared straight ahead, as if both of them had suffered a time warp and were in the throes of suspended animation.

Logan finally, reluctantly, dropped his arm from Whitney's waist.

"Well…"

A shudder went down her spine. She was in big trouble. Heap-big trouble.

"When I asked you to put in a good word for me," Logan went on drolly, "that wasn't exactly the word I had in mind."

Whitney pulled away, and flapped her hands as if she were fanning herself. "I'm sorry! It just came out of nowhere. I don't know why I said it. I don't! Logan—I'm sorry. I'm so sorry. I—"

"Don't keep apologizing."

Whitney agonized, and her heart raced. She was shaking all over, and she couldn't stop. She wiped the corners of her eyes, for fear tears would start dribbling out of them. "I know," she choked. "I've made a mess of everything. But when Madeline started talking about this other couple, I kept thinking how good you were with Amanda, and how she needed you—"

"I appreciate *that*."

"—and one thought just led to another. And I thought about how much you wanted to keep her—"

"There's no question about that, either, but—"

"And then I said something that I—" she struck *wanted to* from the sentence, "—thought would fix it."

He nodded, his look an odd cross between benevolent and baleful.

"Omigod, I'm sorry. You'll never forgive me for doing something this stupid. But I'll make it right. You can't begin to understand how sorry I am, but somehow—"

He put his hand up. "Okay, okay. I'll admit, this is one harebrained idea of yours that's startled me, but if I have to hear one more 'I'm sorry,' I'll—"

"Logan, you have to believe me." Desperation rose in Whitney's pleas, her palms were on his chest, imploring him. It provoked him, the fluttery light sensations she was creating near his heart. A part of him wanted to take her in his arms and assure her it was okay. Another part of him wanted to hear her frustration, to take some time and sort this out. "I never intended for things to get so out of hand. I don't know what got into me. I just thought—"

"Yes?"

"That you needed some help, is all."

"Help? I figured help came in the form of *hired* help. Not a helpmate."

That stopped her.

"Don't put it like that," she said defensively. "It sounds so contrived. So sterile."

Without warning she'd turned the tables on him, striking below the belt and wounding his manly pride. He'd been battling *that* conjecture ever since Amanda arrived in their house. "Sterile? I can guarantee you that's not the reason we adopted Amanda."

Whitney's jaw dropped and her eyes widened. "I wasn't asking," she protested. "I wasn't even implying..."

Logan immediately felt like an idiot to have jumped to the wrong conclusion. "Well, I felt, since we are discussing marriage, that I should to set the matter straight. It was Jill that couldn't have children. I am perfectly capable of bringing a little virility to the marriage bed."

Whitney flushed, uncomfortably. "We aren't discussing marriage," she said flatly, "and certainly not the marriage bed."

"It seemed to me you were. Not too long ago, either. Give or take ten or fifteen minutes." Her eyes, dark with indignation, carried the most incredible pinpoints of gold mixed with brilliant shades of blue. He tried to imagine living with her curious looks, seeing her eyes glow after a night of lovemaking, seeing her patiently sort through a pile of Amanda's dirty socks.

"Just because one fanciful idea went zinging through my head—"

"It wasn't fanciful. It was ingenious." He shifted back on one hip, considering, and taking all of her in. Her sun-drenched cheeks, and the tousled look of her hair. She was witty, yet succinct. Compassionate, yet firm. If he had to weigh her aptitude on some kind of marriage-o-meter, he'd give her high marks. Maybe the second time around was a rational compromise, not a passionate declaration of love and expectation. "Whitney. Stop a minute, and think about this. You obviously have Madeline's seal of approval. She changed her tune the minute you suggested—"

"Don't be ridiculous. She didn't endorse me, she warned me."

"Still...Amanda does like you." He saw a crack in her demeanor.

"And I like her. But—"

"And I like you." To be honest, he couldn't bring himself to use the *L* word loosely. Never could, never would. "Like" would be as close as he'd get.

Whitney's mouth worked, but she didn't say anything.

"And I once told you I'd do anything—*anything*—to salvage the adoption."

"Yes, and I told you once I'd do anything to help...but this is completely out of the question, Logan. It's out of the realm of possibilities. It will buy you some time, and I'll go along with that, but—"

"It's not such a bad idea, Whitney."

"Not for you, or maybe even Amanda," she said hotly. Whitney shivered, knowing how much she cared for him, knowing how easily she could be hurt by all this. "But what about me? I've still got a business to run, and bills to pay. I've got my own home, and a life."

Hah. Her home was a one-bedroom condo, and her life consisted of stocking shelves full of teddy bears that other people bought for their own beautiful children. How many times had she looked longingly at a toddler and ached to have her own family? "You're asking me to become involved with your child. Yours. And how would I fit in? Really?" She could see the debate in his eyes, as if he wondered if the idea was plausible...or worth it. "As your helpmate? One that helps you through this mess? Because we certainly aren't soul mates, destined to—"

"We haven't even discovered what the future holds," he said simply. "Maybe we just don't know it yet."

"Logan…" She was thoroughly, completely exasperated by Logan and by herself. The nagging thought of being married to Logan, even for the briefest time, stirred something profound and needy in her. "We'd be doing it for the wrong reasons."

"People get married for a lot less."

"If we make a hasty decision, Amanda could be hurt by it," Whitney argued. Inside, reason and logic grappled with want and need. She wanted Logan, she always had. But to have him come to her, in this way, would be selling herself short. The ultimate compromise. In the past few weeks they had become friends. How could they become lovers? And how would it end? Miserably? With her out in the cold, and he having what he wanted?

"It could work out," he said persuasively, his touch light on her arm, just above her elbow. That damnable smile of his rose a little higher on the left. "I wouldn't beat you, mistreat you, or cheat you," he said gently. "I promise."

The mere thought that they were actually talking about marriage took Whitney's breath away. As much as she wanted him, it would kill her to be married to him in name only. To be so close, and not possess his heart. To have everything be mechanical and polite between them would be her undoing.

"Nice promises. What about love, honor and cherish?" The words were out of her mouth before she could stop them. She was horrified the instant they were uttered, and yearned to recall them.

He paused, his eyes narrowing. It was the most painful moment of Whitney's life. She had never offered herself up to be judged before. She'd always held herself away, and never allowed anyone to smite her with callous words or indifference. She held her breath, waiting.

"It would be easy to honor you, Whitney. And how

could I not cherish someone who made the ultimate sacrifice for me and my child?''

Logan had, effectively, avoided any reference to love. Whitney realized it, but tried not to think about it. There were worse things, she told herself. She had scraped and got by, and survived for years without the love of two parents, and an ex-husband.

The niggling thought crept into her heart that maybe she was unlovable, but she banished the thought, beating it back and into submission, where it would stay in the remotest recesses of her being.

This was like bartering for something you want, she told herself. She had something he needed, he had something she wanted. A home. A family. A place to belong. It made sense.

Her turbulent emotions began to calm, to subside. This was the Logan she knew, and had always secretly loved. This was the Logan she trusted to be fair. "The way you say it, like that, is kind. But it would be a compromise, for both of us, wouldn't it?''

"Marriage is always a compromise, Whitney. From beginning to end.''

"I don't know. I was a failure at that.''

He grimaced. "I don't think that's a fair comparison—and you know it. You were too young, and the deck was stacked against you from the very beginning.''

Logan had that pegged; her troubles with Kevin had started long before they'd married. Kevin had been on the wrong side of right for a long, long time. She had exited the moment she realized his troubled past would bring her down, too.

"I'm not sure we have enough to hinge it on.'' Even to her own ears, her arguments were growing weak.

"We have Amanda, and good intentions.'' Overhead, they heard the shower shut off. Amanda was humming, her childish voice wafted out through the open window. "Why don't we go in and you can see the house. See if you want to change the drapes, or buy new furniture or something.''

Whitney bit back a wry smile. "Cute."

"You know you want to do this, Whit."

She grudgingly lifted a shoulder. "Yeah, well, it could be a whole lot easier than finding that teddy bear."

Logan grinned, and threw an arm around her before pulling her close. With his left hand he smoothed the hair back from her face, before kissing her lightly on the cheek. Whitney's nerve endings went giddy, and the most inconceivable designation somersaulted through her brain. *Mrs. Logan Monroe.*

"And I want you to do this," he urged, whispering against her ear. "Marry me, Whitney. Let's be a family."

"Logan...I..."

"Daddy?" They looked up. Amanda's face was at the window, her hair in damp tendrils around her face. "Is Whitney going to stay for dinner, too?"

Logan's arm around her shoulders tightened. Once Amanda spied them, Whitney expected to be let go, like a faulty piece of merchandise. "Would you like her to?"

Amanda cocked her head, not even blanching at the way Logan's arm encircled her. "Yeah, that would be great. Maybe, before bed, she can finish that story Mommy started for me and never got to finish. I think there are only a couple of chapters left. I know right where we left off."

Whitney's mouth went watery, and her pulse quickened. She had the most overwhelming urge to flee, before it was too late, before she fell in love with this child and, ultimately, lost her, too.

Beside her, she felt Logan momentarily stall out. She guessed it was one more intimate memory to be reckoned with.

"Where's it at?" he asked evenly.

"In the library. I put it in the basket, next to Mommy's favorite chair."

"Well...ask Whitney if it's all right with her."

She was being drawn into this family, without even trying. She wanted it. The whole enchilada. The husband, the
child, the home that said love lives here. Even if it lasted
for just a little while, she wanted it. "It's all right, Amanda.
I love to read. I grew up reading all kinds of wonderful
books. Maybe…maybe we could start reading books together on a regular basis."

The innuendo must have pleased Logan, because he
squeezed her shoulders even tighter. "You look it up, pip,
while I throw something on the grill for supper. Looks like
Whitney's going to be around for a while."

Amanda's animated face disappeared from the window.

They both stood there, staring at the brick and mortar
rising above the garage. Whitney noticed the slightest im-
perfection on the garage doors, as if tennis balls had left
their mark on the paint. One of the stair treads on the deck
was split, and a hairline crack ran through the cement, just
beneath their feet.

Whitney involuntarily put a new spin on an old saying.
Step on a crack, break your lover's back. She didn't want
to move from this spot, not ever. She didn't want anything
to ever jeopardize the hope that surged inside her.

"I guess that's settled, then," Logan said as he pulled
back from Whitney, leaving a cold spot on her back and
shoulders. "Looks like I have a dinner to fix. And later,
after Amanda's in bed, we have a wedding to plan."

Chapter Six

The first time Whitney crossed the threshold into Logan's home, it was knowing she was going to be his wife. The thought was daunting.

She hesitated inside the back door, aware the kitchen and breakfast nook was larger than the entire first floor of her condo. Logan stepped ahead of her to get the steaks and, with his back to her, he pulled plates and glasses from the cupboards.

She was moving in here? As his wife? Incomprehensible.

Logan glanced over at her, his eyebrows lifting. "Everything okay?"

"Yes. Fine." Even to her own ears her voice sounded small, cautious, too polite.

"You can come in." An amused smile played at the corners of Logan's mouth.

Whitney brushed the palms of her hands over her slacks. "So, what can I do for you?" she asked.

"Marry me," he suggested. "Or...were you thinking of something more immediate?" Without waiting for her reply, he extended the tableware to her and nodded toward the round oak table.

"You might want to be careful about throwing that *m* word around," she said, taking the dishes from him. "Someone might hear you."

"Someone's going to have to hear it eventually."

She paused, putting the first plate on the table, then turning it so the design was upright. "When are we going to tell her?"

He shrugged. "I'd say the sooner, the better. Especially under the circumstances."

Whitney's forefinger pensively stroked the wide band on the second plate. "She barely knows me, Logan."

"Well, we don't have a lot of time for a 'getting to know you' scenario, do we?"

She put the second plate on the table, creating a significant pair. "No. Not for any of us, I suppose." When she looked up, their gazes caught and held.

His eyes were dark, unreadable. "Are you scared?" he asked.

"Don't be silly," she admonished briskly. She placed the third plate on the table, acutely aware she'd added another dimension to the mix. "I can handle myself with children. I'm only thinking about Amanda. And what would be best for her."

Logan, who had just taken the steaks from the fridge, tossed them on the counter, then swiveled to lean against the edge. His hips jutted, one rising slightly higher than the other, as if he was intentionally making his posture either reckless, or a little cocksure. "I know what's best for Amanda. *You're* best for Amanda."

"I appreciate the vote of confidence, but...I'm afraid Amanda might—"

"You're not afraid of Amanda's reaction, Whit," he said pointedly. "You're afraid of me."

"Don't be ridiculous," she said, flustered. "I've known you half my life."

"Not like this, you haven't."

There it was—the man-woman thing, all the implications she'd hoped to avoid.

"The part you knew back then, Whit," he went on, "was a kid. The part you're going to marry is one hundred percent, red-blooded, all-American—"

"Daddy!"

The summons made Logan straighten, disrupting his concentration. "Yes, pip?"

"I found the book!"

"Terrific." He uttered the word, but his expression never changed, and he never once tore his gaze from Whitney.

Amanda trotted into the room, her blond hair flying and the book tucked under her arm, her fingertips clutching the spine. "Look. See? This is the one."

"Yup, sure is." He nodded, bending to inspect the beautifully illustrated copy.

Whitney couldn't help it; she laughed out loud, the tension draining from her.

Logan lifted a quizzical brow as he stood, with the book, now hanging open, in his hands.

"No, there's nothing to fear but fear itself," she quoted, shrugging slightly. "Not from a one hundred percent, red-blooded, all-American daddy."

Whitney turned the last page of the book, amused as Amanda inched onto her lap. The child had first pulled a pint-size rocker up next to the wing chair where Whitney sat, but as she became more immersed in the story, she edged closer. Her elbows were firmly planted in the flesh above Whitney's knees, her stomach draped over the arm of the chair as she strained to see the picture.

"'And, heedless of her tattered gown, the prince took the maiden's hand, declaring to his subjects that she would be the princess with whom he would share his lands, and rule his Kingdoms. For years afterward the people spoke of the strange and unusual way the prince found and came to marry his princess.' And that," Whitney read slowly, "is the end of this story, but the beginning of happily ever after."

Logan peered into the library, just as she finished reading. A damp dish towel clung to his shoulder. "What do you think?" he asked. "Did they live happily ever after?" His eyes bored into her, suggesting a double meaning that made Whitney slightly uncomfortable.

"I...don't know. Not exactly. But I think," she said, "that he was a prince who tried to make a wise decision, one that would benefit him, his family and his people."

"And the princess?"

Whitney hesitated. "I think it probably took a while for her to understand how she fit into his life, to understand what he needed most."

"Interesting," he said finally, lifting the dish towel to wipe his hands on a corner of it. "And perfect timing, too. I'm done with the dishes."

"Thank you, Whitney," Amanda said without prompting. She closed the book. "You read really good. I'm glad you could finish this story for me."

Whitney's heart swelled, but when she looked up at Logan his expression had changed. He seemed to look through her, as if another memory troubled his brow.

"C'mon, pip," he said brusquely. "Time for bed."

Amanda's face immediately clouded. "Do I have to?"

"Of course you have to."

"But it's early, and Whitney's here."

"You can see her sometime next week. Tomorrow you have to get up for school."

Surprise registered on Amanda's features. "Really? I can see her next week?"

He nodded. "Yes. Really."

Then Amanda paused, turning suspiciously to Whitney. "You aren't going to be my baby-sitter, are you?"

A ripple of discomfort went through Whitney. "I wasn't planning on it," she said carefully.

"Good," Amanda replied decisively. "Because I don't want you to be my baby-sitter, I'd rather you just be my friend."

Logan's mouth curled in amusement. He'd pulled the towel from his shoulder, and was folding it. "Why's that, pip?"

"'Cause baby-sitters are nice only because they have to be."

"Whitney's not like that. She's nice all the time. Right, Whit?"

A feeling of apprehension washed over Whitney. What if she couldn't live up to Amanda's expectations? Or Logan's? "Don't paint too rosy of a picture, Logan," she warned lightly, trying to smile through her fears. "I try to be a nice person, but..."

"Roses are red, violets are blue," Amanda rhymed, wiggling her backside in time with her poetry, "my dad says you're nice, and I think so, too."

They all laughed, but Amanda immediately turned to her dad. "So when can we see her again?"

"Well...maybe we could have a bonfire on the beach and roast hot dogs. Or go boating again. Or—"

"I have an idea," Whitney interjected. "Instead of taking advantage of your hospitality, why don't you come and see me, and let me entertain you. We could have a...well, how about a teddy bear tea? Maybe where I work."

At the mention of teddy bear, Amanda's mouth blossomed into a smile, and her eyes widened. "A tea party? Really?"

"Mmm-hmm. With special cookies and my special teddy bear friends," Whitney said. Then, to Logan, she added, "It's something I usually host for my customers. But this time around we could make it a private affair. Just the three of us." Whitney knew Logan was reluctant to bring Amanda to her shop, particularly because of the lost teddy bear, but if they were getting married Amanda was going to have to visit eventually; there was no avoiding it.

"Can we, Daddy? Can we go?"

Logan hesitated. Whitney didn't waver, or draw back the invitation. "I guess. If Whitney wants to do this."

"I do. I think it'll be best."

"Okay, then. It's a date."

Whitney picked up her purse from the library table, then glanced at the grandfather clock in the foyer. It had a face that, oddly enough, reminded her of the clock in *Beauty and the Beast.*

"It's getting late, Logan. Almost eleven. I should go."

"No, stay awhile…." He let the implications drift off. "We have things to talk about, and—" his gaze dropped to her unadorned fourth finger, left hand "—newly *betrothed* couples," he emphasized, "should spend some time alone together."

"Don't joke about that," she said lightly. "We both know this isn't a betrothal, it's an arrangement."

He dismissed the suggestion. "Come out on the deck," he said.

Whitney followed him, mildly surprised when he pulled the patio doors back and waited for her to precede him. Overhead, the stars brilliantly punctured a blue-black sky. Crickets sang in the trees, and beacons of light shimmered off the waters of Lake Justice. This, she thought strangely, was to be her new home.

Logan indicated a pair of chairs in the darkest corner of the patio. Whitney took the first. For a moment, neither of them spoke. It was as if, Whitney thought, neither of them knew what to say. Would this be the way of their awkward and unconventional marriage? Strained silence? Polite reserve?

"I suppose," Logan began, leaning back in the chair and looking out between the rails of the deck, to the water lapping against his private beach, "that we should have some kind of a wedding."

He made it sound like an obligation. A duty. "We don't

have to do anything special on my account," Whitney said, trying to put as much conviction in her voice as she possibly could. "We've both been married before. Under the circumstances, a celebration like that—"

"Whitney. I just meant something instead of a Justice of the Peace, or going to the courthouse or something."

"Oh."

"That stuff always leaves me a little cold. Like you're making it legal, but..." He shrugged, leaving the explanation hang.

"We could do a small wedding," she suggested, darting a look at him, and wondering how he would react. "Just something simple."

"Fine. I think it would be better."

"A small cake, and maybe some flowers. A few friends."

He nodded. "If we have people, we'll have to have a dinner, though."

"Well...if you don't want—"

"No. I think we should." He paused. "I can make arrangements for that at the country club. They're good at receptions."

The suggestion took Whitney's breath away. She had never been inside the gates of the country club, and Logan was suggesting they host their wedding reception there? "It would be short notice, though."

He waved away her warning. "They have a bunch of small conference rooms we could probably fix up for a wedding."

The silence between them lengthened, as each silently imagined their wedding.

"I would like a wedding dress," Whitney admitted longingly. "I never had one before." In the dim light, Whitney could see Logan frown. He turned on the chair, to face her. "Maybe that wouldn't be appropriate. Not at the country club," she said quickly. "Maybe something more subtle. A simple suit, or—"

"No. Do the wedding dress," he insisted, his palm covering the back of her hand, and giving it a light squeeze. "Pick out what you want."

"I know they're expensive, but I could probably borrow something, or maybe—"

"Pick out what you want," he said. "I'll pay for it."

"I didn't mean…." she objected, inadvertently pulling her hand away to protest. "Of course, I can afford to buy my own dress."

"No. Get the dress you want. I want to pay for it." He drew her hands back, slowly, to sandwich between his, and suddenly the old tap dance of desire started running through her veins once again. "We'll only do this once, Whitney, so pick out a gown you fall in love with. You're a bride. My bride. Consider it my gift to you."

Whitney's heart turned over. Her mouth went watery and she didn't know what to say. Though her finances were strained, she hadn't intended to suggest she couldn't provide her own dress. Somehow Logan had turned it all around and, though their union would be nothing more than a marriage of convenience, he'd made her feel special.

But what he said next spoiled it all.

"It can be a quiet wedding, but it can still be nice. And it'll be best to make things look as genuine as possible. For Amanda, as well as my folks. That'll be best, don't you think? To make it look as real as possible."

His remarks leveled Whitney. She knew full well they were marrying because of his predicament with Amanda. Yet Logan was crystal clear on driving one point home: He was hinging their wedding plans on how it would look to Amanda and his parents.

Where, she wondered, did she and Logan fit in?

Chapter Seven

Logan and Whitney agreed on one thing: they'd tell Amanda about their impending marriage Sunday afternoon, at the teddy bear tea. In the days leading up to it, Whitney was a basket case, making sure that every detail was perfect. Past experience confirmed all children loved Teddy Bear Heaven, but she was also acutely aware they typically came in for a toy—they didn't have to face the news Amanda would.

She wondered how Amanda would react—and bought an extra box of chocolate Ding-a-Lings, hoping a little chocolate might sweeten the fact that, no, Whitney was not going to be her baby-sitter, but her stepmother.

Or, technically, her adoptive mother.

Or…was it her foster mother?

In a way, she supposed none of the politically correct terms mattered. She was a fill-in. Like the bride in an arranged marriage, Whitney was the intended mom in an arranged family…and that was okay. It would give her all she'd ever dreamed of, if only for a little while. Yet, for as long as it lasted, she'd be part of something that would stretch to infinity. Her name would be indelibly written on a marriage certificate linking her forever to Logan Monroe.

The thought gave her shivers, and goose bumps raised on her arms. As long as she could remember she'd been smitten by Logan—his smile, his charm, the dimple in his chin, the smooth, clean cut of his hair. She was going to be with him. His partner, his friend.

Would they be lovers?

Well, superhero, came the flip reply, *your mission, should you choose to accept it, is to whisk Whitney Bloom away, and into your bed.*

Both the uninvited question and the lightning-quick response torpedoed through her brain, leaving Whitney weak with longing, flush with desire.

So much was happening. Too much. She glanced at the clock, then across the room, to make sure nothing was out of place, that everything was perfect. *They'd be here in five minutes. Five.* Anticipation and anxiety did a tango in the pit of her stomach.

Suddenly she spied the *Brides* magazine lying open on a table, and the tango tripped into a terrible imitation of the two-step as she scurried to get it, then hide it before either Logan or Amanda saw it. Just then, the bell over the door tinkled. Whitney jammed the magazine beneath a dozen teddy bear bath mats.

She looked around the display to see Logan holding the door open for Amanda. The child was a faceful of smiles, her hair drawn back with a dozen iridescent tiny butterfly clips.

Logan, just as tall and handsome as Whitney remembered when he'd first walked through that door, looked equally pleased to be here.

"Whitney!" Amanda exclaimed. "This is your store? Do all these teddy bears belong to you?"

"Sort of," Whitney answered, smiling down at Amanda's incredulous, wide-eyed enthusiasm. "I'm like their caretaker, really. I keep them for a while and take care of them. Until someone comes along who wants a teddy bear to love."

"Wow. You must like teddy bears even more than me." Amanda twirled between two glass shelving units, one filled with ceramic figurines, the other with teddy bear tea sets.

"Whoa, pip, slow down," Logan admonished, catching her by the arm. "You might break something."

"Don't worry," Whitney assured, "there's nothing valuable at that level."

"Still...."

"Look, Daddy, everything's got teddy bears on it."

"I know."

Amanda pointed to the picture frames, the desk sets, then the bath mats. Whitney cringed, wondering if her secret fantasies would be discovered. She didn't want Logan to think she was taking this wedding thing too seriously. She had, after all, earmarked a few pages of appealing ideas. "Did you see what's back here?" Whitney asked, moving the group away from the bath mats and to the shelves of stuffed bears in the back of the room.

Amanda stopped, standing stock-still, her mouth firming into a fine, wide O; watching her reaction, Whitney and Logan exchanged amused glances.

"Somehow," he said quietly, "I think you've already won her seal of approval."

Whitney could barely squelch back a smile. Her confidence rose, then soared as Logan reached for her hand. The touch was electric, gratifying.

"I had a teddy bear once," Amanda announced solemnly.

Reminders of the past, like old ghosts, surged in the room. Logan fingers stiffened, and he pulled away, slightly, from Whitney.

"You carried it with you everywhere, didn't you, Amanda?"

Amanda's excitement visibly dimmed. She nodded, her mouth firm.

"Do you think," Logan went on carefully, "that you'd like to replace it someday?"

"Someday," she said tonelessly, "but not today."

Forebodings of rejection welled in Whitney. What if the reminders, for both Logan and Amanda, were too great? What if the child's memories of her foster mother were too complicated to overcome?

Whitney chose to jump into the fray. "I've always found, Amanda," she said, "that when I've lost something, I can't ever replace it. Not really. Not even if it's exactly the same. But something else comes along, and somehow, when you least expect it, you discover you can love it just as much as something you loved before. Only in a different way."

"Maybe." Amanda still stared straight ahead, thoughtfully gazing at the dozens and dozens of carefully arranged bears.

Logan, whose expression had been guarded, tilted his head down toward Whitney and, letting go of her hand, mouthed a silent, thank you.

"Amanda, look at this," he said, deftly changing the subject, and indicating the small-scale table and chairs, the dainty tea set. "I think Whitney went all out on your account."

Amanda turned to see it, and immediately giggled. "Oh, my goodness! It's just my size. How are you going to fit, Daddy?"

"I was just wondering that myself," he answered drolly.

"He'll have to scrunch up his legs," Whitney predicted, ushering them to the festively decorated table. "I hope you brought your appetite. We have luncheon sandwiches, cookies, and of course, my special red tea."

"Red tea?" they said in unison.

"Fruit punch," Whitney confided, pulling out chairs for them to sit. When Logan dubiously eyed the miniscule chair, Whitney said, "It's okay. They're handmade and guaranteed to hold 350 pounds. Amanda? Would you like to pour?''

Amanda did the honors and the three of them talked about how Whitney had started her teddy bear business. She entertained them with stories about some of her funniest customers, and some of her most memorable experiences.

Amanda used a paper napkin to wipe the cookie crumbs from her mouth. ''Wow, you're really something, Whitney.''

Logan's mouth quirked. ''She is, isn't she, pip?''

Amanda nodded. ''You always have nice friends, Daddy, but Whitney's special.''

Whitney felt warm heat suffuse her cheeks; the praise was so unexpected. She'd only been trying to make Amanda feel comfortable, she hadn't really been trying for brownie points.

''Amanda, I think you're right about Whitney being special. I've felt that way about her for a long time....''

A desperate feeling plummeted through Whitney's chest. *He was going to tell her. He was going to tell her right now.*

''You know how I told you that Whitney and I have known each other for a long time?''

''Mmm-hmm.''

''Well, I know we haven't seen each other much these past years, but we were talking the other night and we realized that we want to spend even more time together.''

''That's okay with me,'' Amanda said, as if the matter were of little consequence. She picked up another Ding-a-Ling.

''I want to marry Whitney,'' he emphasized, ''and make her my wife.''

Whitney held her breath. Amanda set the Ding-a-Ling aside.

Hearing Logan utter the words, so calmly, with such sincerity, made Whitney go all fluttery inside. Yet she knew her hopes, her dreams, could be dashed in an instant.

"You're going to marry Whitney?"

"I'd like to, yes."

Both adults straightened, intuitively knowing the next question would be, "But what's going to happen to me?"

"She could come and live with us. You and me."

Whitney's heart thrummed so wildly she couldn't trust herself to speak.

Amanda broke into a relieved smile. "Then she wouldn't be my baby-sitter at all, would she? She'd be my—" she broke off, at a loss of words.

"After the adoption's final, she'd be your mother."

"Oh, wow. Then I'd have both a mom and a dad. And that would make Madeline happy, wouldn't it?"

"I'd think so, yes."

"Good," Amanda said decisively. "Because she's been kind of an old witch about me having a mom and a dad."

Logan snorted. "That's putting it mildly," he said.

Even though Whitney had to chuckle, she had some concern about Amanda's understanding of the situation. "You know, Amanda," she said, even though I'd be your mother—your new mother—I would never try to replace your mommy in heaven. I want you to know that.

Amanda's eyes grew momentarily sad. "I guess I understand. It would be like having two mothers."

"Sort of. Yes."

"You won't really be the same?" Amanda asked.

"No. But I'll try my best to make us a family," Whitney said assuringly.

Amanda considered the situation, then demanded, "Well, when are you gonna get married?"

"Probably right away," Whitney answered. "If that's okay with—" She broke it off, instinctively knowing she shouldn't let Amanda have too much say in the arrangements.

"With all the things we have to do to get ready for it," Logan filled in. "Maybe a couple of weeks."

"Where?"

"We haven't decided that."

"We have to find a place," Whitney explained. "Even though it will just be a small wedding."

Logan glanced around the room, "We could even get married here," he said, "the place where we first—"

Whitney raised her eyebrows. "Met?" she asked.

"No." He vehemently shook his head. "Rediscovered each other."

"Could you? Could you get married here?" Amanda pleaded. "It would be so neat."

"It would, wouldn't it?" Logan agreed, his eyes drawn to the teddy bears lining the walls. "There is something about this place, Whit. It's hopelessly romantic."

Whitney's jaw slid off center. Never in her wildest imagination did she ever think she'd hear Logan say something like that. *He used words like romantic?*

"Of course it would be a lot of work for you, but can you imagine, getting married here, with all the exquisite little details you created, all the teddy bears looking on, all being in attendance?"

The idea was appealing, yet...

Whitney's life was wrapped up into her shop, it was her life, her refuge. She considered for a moment, realizing if the marriage didn't work out, it could eventually cast a blight on her workplace. She couldn't imagine coming in, not on a daily basis, and working around nagging memories, lost hopes and dreams. Still...sometimes things in life were a trade-off, just like putting one teddy bear behind you and accepting another.

"It wouldn't be too much work," she said bravely. "There'd be plenty of room if some of these displays were moved."

"We could still have the reception at the country club," he said quickly.

Whitney drew a deep, shaky breath. They'd just moved one step closer to making this a reality. "Then, okay. It's here."

Amanda walked down an aisle, tentatively touching a few teddy bear paws. It occurred to Whitney the child looked worried. "Do you think…" she asked hesitantly, "…that my mommy in heaven would say it is okay to be married here?"

Whitney quickly glanced over at Logan and saw his lips twitch. Amanda's response *was* cute, she conceded silently. Amanda needed to know her mommy in heaven would approve of everything that had happened so quickly.

"I know she would, Amanda," he said. "She'd say it is a very, very special place for us to become a family."

A look of relief passed over Amanda's face.

"And," he said dramatically, twisting slightly on the tiny child's chair to reach into his pants' pocket, "I have something to make it official." He extended a blue velvet ring box, then flipped open the lid.

Whitney's breath caught and lodged in the back of her throat. The ring was exquisite, with a large round diamond, flanked by a half-dozen blue sapphire baguettes. "Oh… my…I—I didn't expect that."

Logan looked pleased, a smile turning the corners of his lips. "Why not? Why should this be such a surprise?"

"Well…I just thought, with such short notice, that if we managed wedding bands, that—"

"You deserve the best, Whitney. But, if you don't like it, we can—"

"Are you kidding?" she managed to say. "I love it, it's…"

"It's probably a little big," he admitted, grinning.

Whitney suddenly felt awkward. She didn't know if she should reach for it and put it on, or simply admire it. She didn't know what the protocol was for accepting diamonds and gold from an old friend turned prospective husband. "It's…lovely, and I hardly know what to say."

"You can say you want to try it on," he suggested.

"I do."

Logan cocked a devilish brow at her, his grin widening. Taking the ring from the box, he extended it, then stopped to catch Amanda's eye. "I think you ought to help me put this on, don't you, pip? I mean, we're all in this together. Sink or swim, for better or worse, and all that stuff, huh? For now and forever, amen."

Amanda giggled, and reached over to help him slide it onto her finger.

"I've never had anything so beautiful in my whole life," Whitney said.

"It's a promise," Logan replied, "and promises are supposed to be beautiful."

The words, so confidently spoken, seemed genuine and Whitney nearly lost herself in the magic, in the idyllic, breathless wonder of the moment they were creating. But, like a serpent that raised its ugly head, she severely reminded herself not to get caught up in the illusion; she was getting married to Logan for Amanda's sake, for that and nothing more.

"This is beautiful," she said, "and I will cherish it. Always."

"Well, I think we really should celebrate," Logan declared, "and with something more than red tea." He stood. "I left a little package just inside the front door." He turned to get it and came back with a bottle of sparkling grape juice, and a gift box of a dozen champagne flutes. "I hope you don't mind if I pop the top in here? We might end up christening a few of these bears and put a dent in the drop ceiling," he warned.

Whitney shook her head. "Pop that top, and put a few memories in this place, will ya?" she joked.

In moments, Logan had peeled the foil back and uncorked the bottle. Amanda clapped her hands when the cork bounced off the ceiling. Whitney dabbed at the foam running down the side of the bottle with an old towel, then she extended two glasses, and a third, "And for you, too," she said to Amanda.

They raised their glasses. But Amanda stopped them cold.

"Aren't you supposed to kiss or something?"

Whitney literally saw a jolt of surprise shimmy up Logan's spine. Suddenly he was at a loss for words. They had never kissed each other in front of Amanda before. Frankly they had never kissed each other period.

"I...I think that's after," Whitney said uncertainly, pausing to study the bottom of her glass.

"Oh." Amanda didn't look convinced.

Whitney raised her glass; Logan and Amanda followed suit. They each took a sip, silently wondering what to do next.

"To our marriage, and a new life," Logan said, "for the three of us." He leaned over, obviously intending to brush Whitney's cheeks with a kiss.

"On the lips, Daddy."

Whitney went weak, right down to the tips of her toes. She wanted to close her eyes and savor the moment. On the other hand, she wanted to see what was coming.

Logan paused, then set his glass down, on the child-size table. He took Whitney's from her hand, and placed it beside his. "We have instructions to do this right," he said huskily. "I think we better comply."

Whitney insanely wondered if she could kiss through a smile.

Logan's mouth swooped down on her, and she discovered she could—and she did. His taste was slow, provocative. His arms looped her waist, his hands on her lower back, drawing her closer, deepening the kiss. Whitney's eyes involuntarily closed. She melted against him, letting the sensations of touch and taste drift through her body. He expertly parted her lips, delving inside her with a probing tongue. The tangy flavor of the sparkling grape juice lingered, mixed with the remnants of raspberry punch. In the recesses of her mind, Whitney surrendered to his quest.

When he gently, reluctantly, pulled free, Whitney's thinking went muzzy, her limbs heavy with want, need.

"A promise," Logan whispered, "sealed with a kiss."

Whitney smiled at him, thinking that this charade was already too much to handle, that she was already falling victim to it. How could one be unresponsive to someone like Logan? He was everything a woman wanted in a man: kind, confident, decisive…and, according to her knees, a very good kisser. "So I guess it's official then."

"Thanks, Whitney," Amanda said, moving in for a hug. "That's the way they do it in the movies."

After Whitney returned her hug, Amanda contentedly turned to the teddy bear puzzle Whitney had offered her earlier. She hummed, as if this wedding thing was a done deal, and happily dumped the pieces out all over the table.

To be freed, but burdened under an avalanche of turbulent feelings, Whitney swayed slightly, even as Logan's arm tightened around her waist. "Hold on a minute," he said, reaching into his pocket for his cell phone. With one hand, he flipped it open and punched in the numbers. If Whitney was surprised that he'd interrupted the moment with a phone call, she said nothing, and tried to collect her wayward emotions.

"Mom?" Logan said. "You busy? I'd like you and Dad to come over to this shop on Beale Street. Something's come up and I want to tell you about it." There was a pause, and Whitney imperceptibly pulled away. "Yes. Right now. Well, I know it's Sunday night, but I figured you guys weren't working, and you'd be free. It's only a few minutes away. The teddy bear store on Beale." Jerking back, Whitney shook her head furiously from side to side. The last thing she wanted today was to meet his parents. "We can grab dinner later if you want. Okay, then. See you in a few minutes."

Whitney, still reeling when he hit the End button on the

cell phone, turned on her heel. "What did you just do?" she whispered. "I can't believe you invited them over here now, not when we just…"

Logan looked mildly surprised, his arm dropping from her waist. "We can't wait any longer to tell them."

"Logan." Whitney couldn't keep the warning from her voice.

"What?"

"Well, you should have asked, for one thing. I'm not sure this is the best time. And I'm not really ready to meet your folks—and here, of all places? Where I work?"

"Where we plan to get married," he reminded. "In two weeks."

"You could have at least given me some warning. It never occurred to me that—"

"Whitney. What's up? This isn't like you to get so defensive."

"Call it nerves," she said, walking away from where Amanda was putting the fourth piece in the wooden puzzle.

"Over what?"

"Well…what if they don't like me?"

He stopped, blinking. "Are you serious?"

"No, I just throw crazy speculation around like that to cause trouble, irritate you, and make myself look like an idiot." His lips twitched. "I'm very serious, Logan. This is going to take them totally by surprise. What if they disapprove? I mean, we've already settled some issues…and I just think that, for today, we should enjoy what we've—" she shot a significant look to Amanda, whose head was still bent over the puzzle, "—accomplished."

"Whitney, here's the thing…I'm going to marry you. With or without anyone's blessing, whether my parents like it or not. I'm a grown man, and I'm capable of marrying the woman of my choice. We're only making an announcement, we're not opening this up and accepting opinions or advice. Not from anybody. Not even my folks."

Logan's vehement reply soothed some of the anxiety

roiling in her. She hesitated, and let out a deep, calming breath. Then she paused to tuck the foot of one teddy bear back on the shelf.

"I probably overreacted," she said apologetically, facing him. "I know they're your parents…I guess I'm just not used to accounting to anyone, not since I've been alone for so long. And I just assumed that you'd have second thoughts if they—"

"Second thoughts? I don't think so. We both know why we're doing this."

The declaration was clear. He was marrying her to keep his child, and he'd let nothing stand in the way of that.

Their gazes caught, and held. They were but steps from each other, but their hearts stretched, molding and flexing nearer each other, within the constraints of time and the legal issues that had been imposed upon them.

Whitney steeled herself, convincing herself this was the last real hurdle she'd have to face before the wedding.

A rap at the door startled them. Even Amanda broke her concentration, swiveling on her seat. Logan moved to the door and Whitney, woodenly, followed him. She put the bravest smile on her face that she could muster.

"Hi!" Logan's mother breezily greeted, sweeping into the room. She wore her usual attire: khaki pants and a no-nonsense golf shirt. "So what's up? What's going on? I swear, Logan, you're worrying us. You never make demands on our time like this."

Logan ignored his mother's questions, and shook his father's hand. "Hi, Dad. Glad you could join us on such short notice." His father nodded, perusing the room and Whitney with an all-inclusive look, before awkwardly patting Amanda on the top of the head. "I'd like you both to meet Whitney Bloom." Reaching back and behind him, Logan snagged Whitney's wrist and brought her forward into the little circle they created.

"Hello," his mother said politely.

"Whitney," his father said.

"Whitney, this is my mom and dad, Walter and Yvonne." Whitney shook their hands, but had the distinct feeling the greeting was obligatory. "Whitney and I graduated high school together."

"You did?" Her mother looked surprised, narrowing her eyes, as if she could conjure up a recollection of Whitney. "I don't remember you, dear. You weren't one of the cheerleaders, were you?"

Whitney blanched; all the cheerleaders in Melville were handpicked from only the most influential families.

"Mom," Logan chided, "you didn't know most of the kids I went to school with. I think you were working on buying the marina then."

"Oh." Yvonne shrugged. "Maybe so. But I noticed them at the football games."

"I wasn't into cheerleading, Mrs. Monroe. I did other things, like the yearbook and the student senate."

"How nice," Yvonne said hollowly.

"Um, look," Logan began, "I know this is a little unexpected, but we wanted you to come over tonight because—" he sidled closer to Whitney, tentatively slipping an arm around her shoulders "—we have something we wanted to tell you. We just reconnected a while back and…" He cleared his throat. "We're getting married."

Neither Yvonne nor Walter Monroe changed expressions.

"We're going to be a family!" Amanda chimed in, wiggling between her grandfather and Logan.

"This is rather…sudden, isn't it, Logan?" his mother remarked.

"Not if you know Whitney."

With all eyes on her, Whitney momentarily felt as if she were on display. She guessed she should say something brilliant, but nothing came to mind. She did the next best thing, and extended her hand, showing them the exquisite diamond-and-sapphire engagement ring. "No one is as surprised as I am," she admitted. "Logan gave it to me tonight, and he was so convincing—and Amanda was so excited—that I couldn't say no.'' She smiled, effectively avoiding telling them the marriage had been her harebrained idea. ''It's such a lovely ring that I'm just astonished. I never expected this.''

The first glimmer of acceptance crossed Yvonne's face, her eyes softened and her mouth relaxed into a slim smile. ''It is lovely. I've always said my son has good taste, and he never pinches pennies on the things he wants…and he's always known what he wants.''

''So when is the big day?'' Walter asked, taking Whitney's hand and nodding approvingly over the ring.

''Two weeks from today,'' Logan announced. ''Can you clear your schedules?''

Yvonne pulled back. ''That's awfully quick,'' she said. ''Not for us. But for you. Are you sure you can be ready in two weeks?''

''It'll be small,'' Whitney conceded. ''Here. At my shop. With you and a few friends.''

''Here?'' Yvonne looked incredulous. ''At a store?''

Walter chuckled, and looked around. ''Yeah. You know, that'll be kind of cute.''

Whitney knew, from the tone of his voice, that Walter wasn't being facetious.

''We'll have the reception at the country club,'' Logan said.

His mother visibly relaxed. ''Well, okay then,'' she said approvingly. ''But I want you to know that I'll be happy to help you with the preparations in any way I can. We may as well make this as normal as possible.''

Whitney froze. Omigod, she thought, the woman *knows*.

Chapter Eight

"**Y**our mother knows why we're really getting married," Whitney said to Logan the following evening. Amanda was at a friend's, and it provided a rare opportunity for them to discuss the wedding plans.

"What do you mean?"

"The way she said that, about making the wedding normal."

"Whitney, she only meant with the small time frame, and everything there is to do—"

"No, she didn't. She knows you're doing this for Amanda, Logan."

"People get married for a lot of reasons. None of them necessarily have to pass parental inspection."

His answer didn't make her feel any better. "I didn't mean we needed their approval. I just thought you should know that I'm aware she knows...that we're..."

Logan cocked his head at her. "Is this one of those he said, she said, we know, they know, sort of things? The kind of stuff women dwell on and worry about and make a big deal out of?"

"Logan! I'm not making a big deal out of anything, I'm just—"

He chuckled. "Well, I'm just asking," he protested. "Because if it matters to you I'll endure it, if not—"

"It doesn't. Not really," she said.

"Mmm. Well, I've got one for you. Mom said you appeared to be a lovely young lady."

"She did?" Stunned, Whitney stared at him. Then she glanced down at the engagement ring. It seemed to wink at her. Without waiting for his answer, she said, "I think your dad thought you went overboard on the ring. I could see it in his eyes."

"No…he was probably a little jealous that he never took the time out of his schedule to do something like that for my mom. Not that she would have wanted a ring like that anyway."

"No? Why not?" It crossed Whitney's mind they might think she was a gold digger, someone who married their son for who he was, not the man he was.

"Mom's never been too much into anything but business. She would have wanted a larger inventory at the marina or the dealerships instead." He turned the sheet Whitney had torn from the *Brides* magazine, to study the centerpieces she hoped to duplicate. It was some frothy concoction with a lot of tulle, and some flowers in a white wicker basket. Whitney said she wanted to add a teddy bear to the whole shebang. He tried to envision it, but his thoughts were on his parents. "My mom barely had time to work me into her schedule."

"She's a very straightforward person," Whitney said. "I can see that."

Logan nodded, his look distant. "I think I always wanted her to be just a little more of a homebody, though. She didn't need to be June Cleaver, but Betty Crocker brownies would have been nice every once in a while."

Whitney chuckled. "I do brownies. My own recipe. Maybe I can fill the void."

Logan's eyes shuttered nearly closed, then he stared down at the menu the country club had suggested. It was everything Whitney was not: cool, sophisticated and just a notch pretentious. "Maybe you can, Whit. I don't know. Maybe you can." He paused. "About this menu for the reception? It's not what you'd choose, is it?"

"Filet mignon and lobster with drawn butter? It's more than I've ever dreamed of—at the same time, at one meal. It's a feast." Then she sobered, "But honestly, Logan, I wouldn't be upset if all we had to serve was sliced ham and cold cuts. I assure you, I'd be satisfied with that." She tried to emphasize that she was marrying him because she cared for him, because she cared for Amanda. All the fancy accoutrements wouldn't change—or affect—how she felt. He was every bit the man that she'd admired from afar, and he still made her blood run hot.

"You're too easy to please," he complained. "But it'll have to be at the country club because it's the best we can do on such short notice. I've arranged transportation there, since we're so close. That way we won't have to bother with cars or anything."

"Oh, Logan, you didn't rent a limo, did you? It's so expensive, and it really isn't necessary."

"Trust me, Whit," he said evasively, "I took care of the transportation."

Whitney assumed he arranged for something special from one of his dad's dealerships. Okay, she wouldn't quibble.

"Whit?" He tapped the guest list. "We forgot someone on the guest list."

"Logan, we're already at—" she leaned against his shoulder, to scan the guest list his mother had put together "—twenty-seven. This isn't going to be a small wedding much longer, and we won't all fit in my shop."

He turned and slipped an arm around her, his elbow and forearm heavy on her back. She could have sworn he was doing that intentionally, and simply waited for her to crumble.

"Just one more," he cajoled. "Please?" He let a heartbeat of silence slip away. "Madeline."

"Madeline?"

"Of course. You know her, and she's Amanda's caseworker so, in a way, she's like part of the family. And I want her to be here, to see for herself that Amanda is okay with this and that we intend to be a family. An honest-to-goodness, genuine family."

His request caught Whitney off guard. She imagined it—Madeline, the woman who held all their futures in the palm of her hand, witnessing the one thing she couldn't possibly undo. It was almost like a coup.

"How can I say no to that one?" she asked, taking the official guest list from him, and penciling in one more name.

Logan grinned. "And one more thing? The dress? Have you found something?"

Whitney hesitated thoughtfully, then pushed the pen and paper aside. "Sort of. But it's kind of overblown. So I'm thinking about it."

"Buy it."

"Not so fast," she warned. "You ought to hear what happened. Because I honestly went in the store to buy something 'country club elegant.' You know. Sleek, chic and sultry."

"Sultry?" He perked up, and inched provocatively closer.

"Mmm." She tried to repulse the crazy stirrings he was eliciting. "But I gave in to this silly whim and tried on this gown that's every little girl's dream. It was just for fun—but I ended up really liking it. It's got sequins and pearls, and a big skirt, and a train, and a neckline that goes—" she attempted to trace the heart-shaped neckline for him "—like this."

He reached over, with his left hand, and followed the path her fingertips had taken.

Through her thin blouse, his touch sent a light, fluttery sensation over her shoulders and onto the tops of her breasts. "Like this?" he repeated, tracing the imaginary neckline a second time.

"Kind of…yes, like that." Her voice had dropped to a whisper. She knew she should move away before she forgot everything she was talking about. But her body willed her closer. "It's…" she struggled to say the words, watching as his eyes skimmed her breasts, to the outline he was creating. The summer-light blouse left little to his imagination. Her breasts peaked, her nipples growing hard and round against her next-to-nothing bra. Logan's fascination with her involuntary response made her draw closer, to shield the intimate details of her body. "It's…it's, um, off the shoulder…"

"Hmm?" His gaze flicked up at her.

"The dress. I'm telling you about the dress."

"Buy it," he said decisively, sweeping the paperwork aside and moving closer to kiss her. He claimed her mouth, sending tiny, darting butterfly kisses between her lips and onto her tongue. Desire ebbed and flowed. They melded together, breathlessly clinging to each other. Finally Logan pulled away. "Buy it," he said hoarsely, "and send me the bill."

They had settled all the details. Whitney would move into Logan's home immediately following the wedding. With their schedule, they couldn't manage a honeymoon, not the kind he supposed he should offer her. But he'd tried to make everything look authentic and, he guessed, from the outside, it did appear so. Sometimes, in the flurry of activity, he almost forgot that he was a widower, marrying for a second time. He almost forgot that these were not the first time jitters he was experiencing, but rather the sexual pull of attraction, the growing bond of friendship, between a consenting woman and a very lucky man.

He was lucky. Incredibly lucky. To find someone as kind, intelligent and good-natured as Whitney, someone who was willing to put her feelings aside, for him and his child.

Thinking of her that way made him feel guilty. As if he wasn't doing enough to make her happy. He sometimes thought of her, reading to Amanda, and the way she read that "happily ever after" part.

His chest grew heavy. Life really wasn't about "happily ever afters." It was about muddling through with someone you were willing to take a chance on, someone you thought you could share your hopes and your dreams with. The thing was, every time he wanted to talk to Whitney, really talk, something stopped him. Like there was this little voice in his head that told him to cut it out, to stop getting close, because you never knew what would happen. It was like these internal brakes kept coming on, yanking him back to the past, challenging his right to go into the future.

He kept reminding himself what he really wanted was a family. It was all he'd ever wanted. Growing up, he'd envied other kids who had brothers and sisters to play with, even to fight with. He'd envied other parents who had gone on picnics or to the drive-in. The only place his folks had ever gone was to the dealerships.

Even as he knew Whitney would unselfishly give him his dream, he wondered if he could really have a future with her. Sure, they were doing this for the right reasons. But marriage needed some bond beyond one small child.

They could joke together, and laugh together...and things were pleasant enough when they were together.

But...something...something deep inside him balked at giving too much of himself away.

He wanted to take her to his bed, there was little question about that. She was a desirable woman and he felt every inch the masculine man when he was at her side. He felt protective and macho and...passionate. Yes, rather damn passionate.

And that would make a mess of things, wouldn't it?

If he was a gentleman he'd do the right thing, and let her make the first decisions about the intimacy they'd eventually share. Given what he was getting out of it, he couldn't very well demand a plethora of sexual favors.

Besides, if he thought this over rationally, and given the timetable of this courtship, nothing they did really fit into an acceptable time frame anyway. So they could take their time with wedding night bliss and all that. It would probably be wiser to do so anyway, because he sometimes thought he was rushing her. As if some kind of rabid passion would fix what they weren't honestly bringing to the marriage bed.

All of it plagued him. All of it. The way he was drawn to her, the way he liked every little thing about her. The way people's eyes widened when he told them he was getting married, the way he had to endure their probing questions or their teasing. The way he wanted to enjoy it; the way he couldn't.

The way everyone assumed he was moving on with his life; the way something deep inside prevented him from doing just that.

"Daddy...?" Amanda said, interrupting his thoughts.

"Yes, pip?"

Amanda stood just outside the library door, as if reluctant to intrude. "I have something to ask you."

"Okay." He swiveled around in his desk chair and propped his elbows on the desk.

"Is Whitney going to be the boss of me?"

Logan stopped and considered her question. "The boss of you," he repeated. "What do you mean?"

"Like will she tell me when to go to bed, and when to brush my teeth and stuff? Or whether or not I have to eat my carrots?"

He chuckled; Amanda detested carrots. "I'm sure she'll remind you to go to bed. As for teeth..." He purposely leaned back in the chair, as if he were pondering the magnitude of her questions. "Yes, I suspect she might remind you to brush your teeth." He rolled his eyes at her. "I mean, who wants skunky looking teeth anyway?"

In spite of her apparent worries, Amanda giggled. "Skunky looking. Oh, Daddy. You're so funny."

"Mmm," he agreed, "my sense of humor is my best trait. Now, getting back to the carrots, she'll probably say we all have something we don't like, but I doubt she'll make you eat them."

"Do you think?" Amanda inched inside the room, her back to the doorframe.

"I can't say for sure. But I know I heard her say she didn't like broccoli. So it stands to reason that the carrots wouldn't be a problem."

Amanda wandered into the room, then paused at the corner of his desk. She toyed with the paper clips he kept in a glass bowl, letting them *chir* through her fingers. Before Amanda glanced up at Logan from beneath lowered lashes, she let the last paper clip fall back into the bowl. "Do you think," she asked slowly, "that Whitney is really as nice as she seems?"

Logan frowned. "Why wouldn't she be?"

"Oh, I don't know. I just wondered."

"Whitney is a very nice person, Amanda," Logan said, trying to reassure her. "She has been ever since I've known her. In high school, she was never mean." He moved on the chair seat, making his lap available, in case Amanda needed to crawl up and confide her deepest fears.

Amanda sighed, heavily. "I wonder if she yells."

"Whitney? Yell? The only time I ever heard her raise her voice was when she was singing that silly toot-toot song with you in the back of the pontoon." He tried, valiantly, to make a joke of it.

"She did get loud," Amanda allowed, a small smile slipping onto her lips.

questions? I thought you liked the idea of us getting married.''

"I don't know." She lifted a shoulder, her eyes still fixed on the button. "I just wondered if Whitney will change, I guess."

"Change? Like how?" he persisted.

"Like if she'll yell at me and stuff." Amanda's mouth firmed, and her eyes hardened. "Kelly Foster's new dad yells at her."

"He does?"

"Yeah. He seemed really nice for a while too, and then her mom got married to him, and now he yells at her all the time. I heard him."

"Oh. I see." Logan purposely let a second slip away. "I suppose that makes you think about how things could change after Whitney and I get married."

"A little."

"Amanda, Whitney is her own person, she's going to be different from the mother you remember—but that doesn't mean it's going to be bad. Just different."

"She won't do things the way Mommy did them, will she?"

"No. She won't. But I think Whitney's going to make us very happy. She's going to make us a family again. We'll be a dad, and a mom, with a little girl right in between, right where she should be."

Amanda looked up at him, her eyes wide, her smile brave. "I know. I do like her, Daddy. Really. And I'm glad we're getting married to her."

Logan chuckled and hugged her tighter. "I'm glad, too. I think you'll learn to love her, and I think you'll see that we're getting married for all the right reasons."

Staring down into the innocent eyes of his little girl, Logan wondered if he could find his way out of the turmoil he was in and come to convince himself of the same things he'd just told his little girl.

* * *

His parents insisted they have a wedding rehearsal. Whitney wasn't sure why, as they weren't having any attendants, only Logan's cousin, Mike, and his wife, Jan, to fill in as a host and hostess. Amanda would carry a basket of pink rose petals as she stood with them before the minister. It was enough.

While the men moved some of the shelves and arranged the chairs before they went to dinner, Whitney, Jan and Yvonne put the finishing touches on the shop, effectively turning it from Teddy Bear Heaven to "wedding bear heaven."

"Whitney, I think the guest book should be here," Yvonne insisted, moving a small table to the other side of the door. "It's more functional. And don't you have a tablecloth to put on it?"

"I didn't think of that...." Whitney trailed off, momentarily thinking she was in over her head. Her hands trembled, and she wondered for the umpteenth time what she'd gotten herself into. "But I've got an old lace curtain in the back room, we could use that."

"An old curtain?" Yvonne questioned, her voice rising with undisguised disbelief.

"Lace is a wonderful idea," Jan interjected. "It will fit perfectly with this atmosphere. I'll help you find it and we'll make it fit. Besides, who's to know?"

Whitney grinned, realizing she had a friend in Jan. With a few ribbons and some leftover strands of pearls from last year's Christmas tree, they worked to tailor a custom-made tablecloth.

Yvonne stood back, critically studying the effect. "Whitney," she said, "you are ingenious. I can see why my son's taken with you."

The unexpected praise warmed Whitney. "Thank you," she said, "but I have to confess I wasn't sure it would work."

"You're missing something, though." At Logan's remark, both Jan and Whitney turned back, to see what they may have overlooked. "Teddy bears by the guest book and flower arrangement?" he suggested.

Whitney strode to the front counter, to retrieve Byron. "This is the guy," she said. "He's been my best buddy, so I guess he deserves to sit at the guest book."

Logan paused long enough to put the display of teddy bear jewelry he was carrying to the back room on the floor. "So," he said, taking Byron from Whitney's hands to examine him, "is this my best man—or my competition?"

Yvonne rolled her eyes. "For heaven's sake, Logan, you aren't going to be jealous of a teddy bear, are you?"

Logan's gaze slid to Whitney's, the current between them tangible. "If he takes too much time away from my future wife, I may be."

"Oh, come on. Byron's your best man, whether you know it or not," Whitney countered, feigning a pout.

"And that would be, because…?"

Whitney struck a coquettish pose. "Because he's the one guy who always stuck around. Maybe, if it wouldn't have been for him, you wouldn't have walked in this store, and—"

"And found a little bit of heaven," Jan put in, teasing.

Logan intentionally let his mouth curl, and one eyebrow ride seductively higher than the other. But on the inside another war was raging.

That, or a little bit of hell? he silently asked himself, studying Whitney's sultry pose.

How would it be to be married to Whitney, and still manage the delicate balance of their public and private facade? It was so easy to flirt with her in public. But in private? One of the most fascinating things about her was that she was so innocent. She had absolutely no idea she had the capability of turning jeans, worn-out tennis shoes and off-the-rack dresses into seductive garb—and he needed to fortify his defenses. Quickly.

Chapter Nine

The wedding was set for four in the afternoon. Logan told her to be ready twenty minutes before the ceremony and someone would arrive at the condo to pick her up. She would recognize her escort, he assured her.

Beneath her sequin-and-pearl bodice, trepidation frolicked. Fingering the long, slim petals of the orchids in her bouquet, she tried to calm her nerves by taking a mental inventory of all the details she intentionally included in the wedding plans. None of which anyone would notice.

Roses, orchids and baby's breath in her bouquet—symbolic of life, love and children. Something old: her gram's lace handkerchief, folded carefully inside her bra, and placed next to her heart. Something borrowed: Amanda's gold baby ring, which she wore on her necklace, with her teddy bear charm. Something new: the extravagant gown Logan had unflinchingly paid for. Something blue: the traditional blue-and-white garter.

Everything was so perfect Whitney wanted to pinch herself to make sure this was really happening. That she was really marrying the man who had stolen her heart all those years ago, that she would be a mother to his child. She knew it wouldn't be easy, and there were times she almost wanted to wiggle under Logan's skin to learn what he liked, what would make him happy. Sometimes she felt like she just couldn't get close enough to him—and that disturbed her. But she vowed to change it. She silently vowed, as she stood alone at the door of her empty condo, that she would give this marriage her all.

A jingle and a clip-clop clatter at the entrance of her condo community made Whitney strain against the screen to guess what was going on. She couldn't see anything—then a white-and-gold carriage rolled into view. The driver and an attendant sat high atop the bench seat of the exquisite carriage, the driver's white-gloved hands held the reins of the perfectly matched white horses. He pulled back, stopping the pair in front of her narrow sidewalk. People came out of their homes to gawk—men who had been washing cars, turned off hoses and stared; children stopped playing kickball and gazed, awestruck and wide-eyed.

Whitney stood frozen to the spot, fearing she'd make more than a spectacle of herself, fearing this was too much for an ordinary person like herself.

The attendant, decked out in black coat and tails and a high top hat, swung down from the bench seat and strode up the steps and onto the sidewalk. "Miss Whitney Bloom?" he inquired.

Whitney's heart hammered in her chest. She nodded, taking a deep breath.

"Your carriage has arrived."

"I…" She paused, swept away by the gallantry of the moment, by Logan's surprise. "I wasn't expecting this," she said shakily. "I was expecting four wheels and a motor."

The attendant laughed, opening the door for her and offering his arm. "We have the four wheels," he assured. "And our 'motor' doesn't lack for horsepower."

Whitney had to laugh, waiting while the attendant made

sure the door was locked behind her. He stopped for a moment to make sure her skirts and train were carefully arranged. ''Your fiancé,'' he explained, escorting her to the waiting carriage, ''has asked that
you be treated royally.'' He opened the carriage door, to help her inside, and again readjusted her voluminous skirt. ''If there's anything you need….'' The attendant indicated the gold cord attached to a tiny bell next to the driver's seat.

Whitney took in all the details, feeling as if she was floating into the next phase of her life. The tulle of her veil stirred in the breeze, drifting out over the edge of the carriage. Around her, the growing sound of applause echoed through her small community.

''Way to go, girl!'' someone shouted.

''Congratulations, Whit!''

''Best wishes.''

''You make that man behave now, you hear!''

The carriage started swaying, and the horses turned, to whisk Whitney away to her nuptials. Children ran up and behind the carriage, women waved and men winked. Whitney responded, lifting her elbow, to return the farewell with the slightest wave of her hand. She turned on the seat, looking back and waving, as the carriage moved out and onto the main thoroughfare.

The driver and attendant nodded to gawkers. They stopped traffic in downtown Melville, and drew a crowd. Shopkeepers came to stand on their doorsteps, and tourists snapped pictures. Even as her anxiety grew, and her hands shook, Whitney's smile widened.

She felt like Cinderella.

In twelve short minutes they were outside her shop. Logan, in a dark tuxedo and wine-colored cummerbund, waited like a sentinel at the door. His hand rested lightly on Amanda's shoulder, but his eyes were fastened on his bride. When the carriage pulled to a stop, he stepped away from Amanda, blocking out the dusty-rose color of her long gown.

The attendant swung down, "Your bride is safely delivered, sir."

"Thank you." Logan waited until he unlatched the door, and helped her up from the velvet seat and down onto the cement. Then the attendant gave her to Logan as carefully as a father would give away his prized possession.

Whitney swallowed, afraid she would choke with unspent emotion. "You should have told me," she managed to say, looking up at Logan while she tightened her hold on his arm, feeling, even through the twill of his tuxedo, the strength throbbing beneath.

"What? And spoil the surprise?" he asked, his mouth curving like the cat that ate the canary.

"It was wonderful, Daddy!" Amanda gushed, running to his side but peeking up at the huge, stamping horses.

"It was," Whitney agreed, turning against his shoulder for a last fleeting glimpse. "Wonderful. Magical." She tried to take it all in, to sear every detail of the moment in her memory.

"It's not over," Logan said, drawing her back against him. "It's a day that's just beginning."

A day, Whitney thought. One day of magic, and then their life would turn to the day-in-day-out reality of the commitment they were about to make. Part of it scared her, and awed her. There was only one thing to do, she told herself firmly, enjoy the day and what it brought. Make the most of every memory.

"We will be prepared to carry you to the reception after your nuptials, sir," the attendant said. "And we've arranged for the photographs to be taken on the country club lawn."

"Thank you," Logan said again, as faint strains of music wafted from Whitney's shop.

Logan and Whitney had agreed not to have anything as traditional and strident as the wedding march. In the small confines of her shop it seemed prudent to have the mere

hint of music, and they chose the theme from Franco Zef-
firelli's *Romeo and Juliet.*

The moment Whitney placed her foot on the threshold,
she regretted the choice.

*Star-crossed lovers. Families who were at odds. Ill-fated
romance.*

Guests, at the suggestion of the minister, stood and
turned to the open doorway. Amanda preceded them, walking ahead to stand in the front, to the spot they had chosen
for her. Whitney looked beyond the guests she didn't know,
mostly close friends and relatives of Logan's, to the flick-
ering candles on the table. Instead of the traditional tapers
for the bride and groom, Logan and Whitney had agreed
there should be three, one to include Amanda. Perhaps,
now, it looked strange. Yet, when the ceremony was over
they would light the single pillar, symbolizing that they
were a family united.

Logan took the first fateful step, putting a gentle pressure
on her arm, and imperceptibly tugging her into the building.
The setting had been transformed. Gone were the displays
and end caps of merchandise and in their place were me-
ticulously arranged chairs and a white runner. Yvonne had
picked out the floral arrangements and they were exquisite.
At the foot of each, she had placed a teddy bear. The table
before which they would stand was at the back wall, before
her rows and rows of attentive teddy bears. Every row was
strung with an ivy and white rose garland.

Logan chuckled, then whispered down to her, "Looks
like your guest list outnumbered mine."

Whitney bit back a small, embarrassed smile.

The ceremony was brief. The minister included pertinent
remarks about both the bride and groom, the sanctity of
marriage, and the vows.

The moment she said them, Whitney felt giddy but then
she felt as if Madeline's eyes were boring into her back,
threatening to put an end to their charade. Fortunately, Logan caught her attention, and brought her back to his world,

encouraging her with the hint of a smile, the touch of his hand.

He slipped the wedding band into place.

It was over too quickly, but for a while Whitney had succumbed, losing herself to the illusion they had created.

Madeline was one of the first to congratulate them. Her smile was guarded. "Best wishes," she offered. "I swear, Whitney, this is just like a storybook wedding. Getting married in here reminds me of being inside a gingerbread house."

Whitney laughed at the comparison. "We go back to being plain old Teddy Bear Heaven on Monday. I'm sure it will take me all week to get things back to normal, too."

"What? You're not taking a real honeymoon?" Madeline inquired, her eyes unusually bright.

Whitney's antennae went up, wondering if Madeline was intentionally trying to catch them in a lie, and expose the real reasons behind their marriage.

"We're going away next weekend," Logan said quickly, smoothly. "Just a quiet getaway." He neglected to mention that their "romantic" weekend away would include Amanda, and a toy show where Whitney would actually combine a little business, a little pleasure. "We're both taking a few days off next week instead. We want to finish moving Whitney into the house, and take some time on the beach."

"Really?" Madeline purred. "Then I suppose you won't want me dropping in unannounced."

Whitney didn't observe one crack in Logan's composure. "You're welcome any time," he said.

Madeline laughed, then winked. "Be prepared. I just might take you up on that invitation."

Dread prickled over Whitney's scalp. What if they had gone through all of this to only lose Amanda? When Madeline moved on, she leaned into Logan. "Did she mean that?" she whispered.

"We'll find out, won't we?" he said easily, reaching

over to grasp his cousin Mike's hand, and to accept more congratulations.

There was no time to dwell on it, and the minutes evaporated into quick introductions and hasty poses for family photographs. Soon Yvonne was herding them to the door, reminding them they could dawdle at the reception.

Outside the carriage still waited, and Whitney stepped onto the sidewalk with her arm looped through Logan's. The attendant greeted them, ushering them around to the back of the carriage. "For your approval, sir," he said.

On the back of the carriage hung a large sign, topped by clusters of real carnations and twining ivy. Just Married, it read.

"Yes," Logan said approvingly, "I think this announcement is definitely appropriate."

Walt, who was in charge of the family camera, insisted they pose for a picture. Logan immediately postured like an English gentleman; Whitney plastered a wide smile on her face and pointed to the "Just Married" sign. Onlookers howled.

"Me, too!" Amanda cried. "Take my picture, too," she insisted, spontaneously joining in the fun, and taking a place next to Whitney. Whitney dropped her pose, and pulled Amanda close, meshing the rose silk of the child's gown with the organza and lace of her own.

The moment was magical, making Whitney truly believe this family thing was possible. It seemed so real, so genuine.

"That was definitely our family portrait," Logan said moments later, as he helped Amanda up into the carriage to sit between them. He grinned over the top of Amanda's head at Whitney. "I think I'll have a copy enlarged, to always remind us of the day we found our way into each other's hearts."

Whitney shivered—she'd come to love the kind way he had of saying things.

Logan reached over Amanda's lap, for her hand, sneaking under the bridal-white bouquet to curl his fingers around her own. "You're a beautiful bride, Whitney. And I'm a very lucky man to have things work out this way. You're going to make a great mom to Amanda, I just know it."

Whitney smiled over the tremulous beating of her heart, imprinting the vision of Logan's profile on her memory. *And what about being a great wife to you?* she silently asked. *Please, tell me that's important, too.*

The driver cracked the whip, mostly for show, and the carriage lurched forward. They immediately hit a small pothole and were jostled from side to side. Amanda squealed, and Logan braced an arm against the velvet-tufted seat.

"Oh, my! Is this supposed to mimic real life?" Whitney rhetorically questioned, slapping a hand to her headpiece to make sure the veil wouldn't flutter behind her and end up beneath the back wheels of the carriage. "A few rough starts, a few bumps in the road?"

"I don't know," Logan said, as he struggled to sit upright. "But I'm riding this out. I refuse to allow anything— even a pothole—to put a damper on the beginning of our life together. And it's going to be a beautiful life, Whitney. I promise you that."

Chapter Ten

Logan made sure that the wedding reception lacked for nothing. Aside from the extraordinary dinner, the waiters offered red wine, white wine, champagne and punch. The country club had arranged for a harpist during dinner, and a pianist after. When they stepped onto the dance floor, Walt followed them to take their first photos as they danced as husband and wife.

Logan, tall and handsome in the tuxedo, turned to Whitney and extended his arms. Trancelike, she floated into them, oblivious to all the onlookers.

"We're about twelve years late, but it looks like I'm finally getting that dance I promised myself in high school," he said, after they made their first sweep around the floor.

"Are you disappointed to be waltzing to Strauss, instead of rockin' and rollin' to some jungle beat?"

He pulled back, feigning mild disappointment. "Whitney. There's always going to be some jungle beat pounding through my veins." A dozen guests started tapping their spoons to their crystal, demanding a kiss. Logan chuckled, then made a show of bending her gently backward and kissing her soundly.

Whitney went weak as his legs sliced between hers. His fingers tautly pressed seed pearls and sequins into the lower part of her back. When the pianist faded into another piece, Logan reluctantly lifted her and pulled away. "See?" he said huskily. "It's that old animal magnetism."

Walt immediately handed Logan the camera, suggesting that since Whitney's father couldn't be there for the daddy-daughter dance, he'd feel privileged to have the honor.

Whitney choked back a lifetime of emotion, regret.

"It's a shame none of your family could come," Walt said easily, after their first spin around the floor.

"I really don't have any family," Whitney said. "My mom travels a lot, and it's hard to reach her so I didn't even try."

"I hope she won't be too upset to miss everything."

"My mom's pretty—" Whitney lifted her shoulders, searching for the right word "—flexible. Who knows? She'll probably send us something from Morocco when she finds out."

"We can't come up with anything that exotic, but both Yvonne and I want you to know that we'd like you to consider us family. Right from the first. None of this first name business. Dad'll do. When you're comfortable with it, that is."

The suggestion took her breath away. He was trying, really trying to accept her and let her be a part of his family. "Thank you," she managed to say. "That's very kind of you. Really. You've both been wonderful, and I want you to know I'll do everything I can to make Logan happy."

"I know you will, dear." Walt nodded and, as the music ended, he handed her safely back to Logan.

In the half-light of the car's interior, Logan glanced over at Whitney. It looked like she was being swallowed alive by her wedding gown. The skirt billowed over the seat and mounded like meringue to the top of the dash. The graceful curve of her shoulders and the slim column of her neck appeared to float above the froth.

She picked at a seed pearl, making him guess she was nervous.

"I can't believe I forgot about a hotel room," he apologized for the second time. "It never occurred to me Mom and Dad would offer to take Amanda. They *never* offer to take Amanda."

Whitney turned slightly. "It's okay. We had other things on our minds."

Logan eased the Lincoln onto the driveway of his home. "Even so, I should have booked the bridal suite at the Willingham."

He pulled around the circular driveway, and parked near the front door. For a moment neither of them said anything.

Yup, this was it, Logan thought facetiously. The big deal. The official wedding night. Whitney was glued to her door handle, he was glued to his. His hormones were throbbing and everything around him was awkward as hell.

"Your father is a very generous man," she said.

Logan smiled down at her. "Why do you say that?"

"He's so kind. He welcomed me into the family, asked me to call him Dad..." Whitney followed Logan's lead for another dance, this time to the hopelessly romantic melody of a popular song. "You know," she said thoughtfully, "he really does remind me of you. Gracious, kind, generous to a fault."

Logan chuckled. "My. You don't have to win me over anymore—we're already married."

"Logan...I only meant—"

"I know, I know. You're trying to get on my good side," he teased. "Know what?" he asked, brushing a kiss across her temple. "It's working, too."

He wondered, vaguely, how many men took a cold shower on their wedding night.

"It does seem strange without Amanda between us, doesn't it?" Whitney finally said.

"I guess. But...well, maybe it's a good thing. I mean we've got to get to know each other all over again, Whit." The tight feeling in his groin had nothing to do with "getting to know her" any other way but intimately. He leaned back, putting his arm on the back of the seat.

He could have kicked himself the moment he made the high-schoolish move. It looked like he was coming on to her. Yet Whitney didn't seem to notice.

"The reception was wonderful. It was very thoughtful of your folks."

"It's important to them to make a statement." He picked up a corner of her veil, rubbing it between his fingers before he pushed it back over the seat, and exposed more of her bare shoulders. "Now Mom feels like she's done her duty and they'll go on, satisfied that they've met their responsibilities."

Whitney turned a little more, and the hollow of her shoulder deepened. Logan imagined his head resting there, so close to her breast, his chin, his cheek, pillowing on the soft mound of her flesh.

"You're sounding cynical, Logan. Especially about your folks."

"It's just—" He shrugged as if the matter were of little consequence "—the way things are." Reaching over, he tuned the radio to an FM station, letting the soft strains of classical music fill the interior. "I hope you weren't overwhelmed by my family. They get a little boisterous, but they mean well. Even my folks, I suppose."

"It was wonderful. All of it."

"Did you feel outnumbered?" he asked.

"Not so much. I've gotten used to being on my own." She shifted the bouquet she still carried, fiddling with a sprig of baby's breath. "Of course, there were times I wished that I had a family."

"Well, you've got one now. Whether you want it or not,

your name's on the dotted line." He tried to tease, but the fact was he had mixed emotions over the whole thing. He never intended to get married so soon. He never intended to feel this way either. "No going back now."

"I guess not. But I can't believe it's over," she said pensively.

"Me, either. I guess this is where we get down to the reality of day-to-day living, huh?"

"I guess."

Her lack of enthusiasm bothered him, as if her back was to the wall and she didn't have any way out. She looked so vulnerable, sitting there in her virginal white, the perfect roses and lilies strewn across her lap.

How could he be thinking of doing what he was thinking to her, for crying out loud? Not *to* her, he severely reminded himself. *With* her.

This was Whitney, for pete's sake. Of course he wanted to. Hot damn, he wanted to. And he shouldn't. He shouldn't even make the move.

But, hell, that's what men and women did together. They made love. It was fun. It was pleasurable. And, most of the time, it was a pretty damn good diversion.

But with Whitney? What if he woke up tomorrow morning and felt as if he'd taken advantage of her?

The hard, crisp lines of his trousers buckled. He ended up feeling just a little bit deflated…and that was a hell of a thing to feel on your wedding night.

"Hey," he said brightly, lifting the door handle, "you hold that pose, 'cause I'm coming around to carry you over the threshold. We've got to get these details right."

He jumped out of the car, grateful when the cool night air struck him. "Yeah, yeah. Cool your jets, Romeo," he muttered, bounding up the front steps to unlock the door and leave it ajar. When he turned back to the car, he took a deep breath, and once again made the conscious decision to put his fate in her hands.

Whitney had already opened the door and was struggling

with her skirts, her bouquet and shoes. She wiggled a stock-
inged foot beneath the hem of her skirt. "I shouldn't have
taken my shoes off," she needlessly explained.

"Here, let me." He took the slippers from her, and cap-
tured her heel in the palm of his hand. "You might, I don't
know…drop them or something…." Easing the pumps
over her toes, he let her push into them. His hand inadvertently inched up her calf, and he was stricken by how curvy
she was—and in all the right places, too. "Now, the other
one…." He reached out to take the second slipper, not
trusting himself to reach into her lap for it. "There. Better?"

"Much. But I can walk."

"Don't be silly. It's tradition. Grooms carry their brides
over the threshold."

"I'm too heavy for you, Logan."

"Let me be the judge of that," he said, sliding an arm
around her lower back and beneath her knees. It was the
way she giggled when he lifted her that made his blood
race. That, and the way she looped her arms around his
neck. "I think," he said, his heavy breathing having nothing whatsoever to do with her weight, "that when I get to
the top, and inside the door, I'm supposed to kick it shut
with my heel."

"Really," she asked, her breath soft against his cheek,
"is that tradition, too?"

"Either that, or I got it mixed up with some movie."
She laughed as he crossed the threshold, briefly tipping her
head against his. The intimacy nearly toppled his plans.
"And a kiss for luck," he suggested, light from the foyer
spilling across them as he shouldered the door shut.

Whitney sobered, her full, kissable mouth parting
slightly. Her eyes were doe soft, and for some strange reason he compared it to that deer-in-the-headlights look. He
didn't want her to be afraid of him. Not ever.

His lips sought hers and, for an instant, he thought he'd
never tasted a woman so sweet, so desirable. Yet, as their

kiss lingered, she slipped from him—her body sliding downward, her toes pointing to the floor, her gown clinging to his rumpled tuxedo, his hands meeting at the small of her back. He pulled away first.

"Whitney…?"

"Mmm-hmm…?"

Her head was on his shoulder and he guessed her eyes were probably closed. "Um…we probably ought to talk."

"Now?"

"Well, yeah, about now. At least about tonight."

"Okay."

"I just want you to know that…" He took a deep, cleansing breath. "I don't expect you to sleep with me. I mean, I know this is kind of sudden and all, and I guess if we wanted to take some time…to, you know, adjust…that it might be prudent. Understandable, even. There's been a lot of stress, a lot of late nights, we've both had a lot to think about…."

Disbelief rippled through Whitney. She couldn't believe what she was hearing. He didn't want to sleep with her. Maybe he didn't even consider her desirable enough to sleep with. Desirable enough to be a mother to his child, but…

She had to think logically. She had to salvage this moment—as well as her pride. "Of course," she said. "A lot of newlyweds postpone their wedding night. It makes sense." *No, it doesn't,* she silently railed. *I want you. I've wanted you for forever. You can't bring me this close and not let me have that one part of you. I want to feel as close as I possibly can to you. I know you don't love me, but I want you to make love to me.*

"Maybe as we settle in…"

Maybe?

"I could put your things in the guest room, if you'd like."

If she'd like? She was destined to be his wife, and the

mother of his child—from the guest room? ''If—if that won't be any trouble,'' she sputtered.

''Oh, no. No trouble at all.''

He headed for the car, to get her train case and her overnight bag. Whitney studied the solid wedge of his shoulders, the ramrod straight steps he made across the foyer. Was that relief she'd seen on his brow—or determination to get through this awkward moment?

She told herself she was doing the right thing, to let him off the hook like that. She was taking the complications out of her life. She was being prudent, proceeding with caution.

Then why, if she was doing all the right things, did she feel so darned miserable on what was supposed to be the most splendiferous night of her life? Did Logan really intend to burst the bubble on their charming little tale of matrimonial bliss—or was he just being an honest-to-goodness, prince of a guy?

Chapter Eleven

Whitney had never imagined a big old bed—especially a queen-size bed—could be so lonely. At first she couldn't sleep, her mind turning over all the events of the day. Later, she couldn't sleep because she kept reminding herself she was in Logan's home, and that he was her husband, and he was sleeping alone, just across the hall.

She wondered if, in bed, he wore pajamas or briefs. Or nothing at all. She wondered if he showered in the morning, or at night. She was certain she had heard his shower running after she'd slipped into bed—and for an extraordinarily long time, too.

It occurred to her that she could get up, in the middle of the night, and look in on him…ask if he needed anything. Warm milk? An extra blanket? A wedding night?

Her imagination had always run a little rampant, giving her courage and hope and a dash of humor when things looked particularly dismal. Anyway, she rationalized, why would she want to give Logan a wedding night now? She didn't even have a decent nightgown. Wedding nights demanded decent nightgowns. Something sexy, yet innocently provocative. Why, she'd been so busy putting this wedding together she hadn't even thought of a nightgown.

Maybe it was better this way. To abstain, until they got the details right.

At 7:00 a.m. Whitney finally heard Logan rattling around, and she immediately got up—but not soon enough to see him go out the front door. Dressed in her favorite slacks and shirt, she immediately went down to the kitchen, determined not to feel like a guest.

Coffee was perking when Logan, in sweats, came in through the back door. Surprised, he fingered the towel looped around his neck. He looked little-boy tousled, in a rugged, manly sort of way. The image tugged at her heart.

"You're up already? Did I wake you?"

"No, I couldn't sleep anyway." She blanched, wanting to kick herself for making any reference to what happened—or hadn't happened—last night. "Probably just getting used to a strange house, that's all. The bed—" *The bed?* What was she saying? "It was a little hard...I mean—I mean, firm." Feeling her face flush, she turned away. "I'm just used to something softer, is all." Oh God, this was getting worse.

"You weren't comfortable. I'm sorry, I thought—"

"No, I was...fine. Really." She stirred the pancake batter, watching him from the corner of her eye as her heart thrummed. "I didn't know you liked to run in the morning."

"Once in a while. It's a good way to—" he shrugged, as if the matter were inconsequential "—clear my head." He paused, leaning back against the doorframe to study her. "I kept thinking about the wedding, and everything yesterday."

"Oh? Me, too." Sinking a hip against the counter, she extended the mixing bowl. "If you want, we can talk about it later over pancakes."

"Sounds good. But I should be taking you out for breakfast. It's your first day, and instead of you slaving away in the kitchen—"

"No, that's okay. I'd rather stay here." He nodded and she carefully set the bowl aside on the countertop. "You don't have to treat me like a guest, Logan. I'm your wife. As goofy as it sounds, I looked forward to fixing you your first breakfast. Getting Amanda off to school for the first time next week. Getting my first piece of mail at my new, address—as your wife."

"It's going to take me a while to get used to the idea of you being my wife," he admitted, pulling himself away from the wall and walking into the room. "I keep thinking of you in chemistry class, with your hair pulled up, and how you wrinkled your nose when your experiment didn't work." Logan cocked his head, his eyes narrowing as he remembered the girl she'd once been. "And then I think about seeing you again in that showroom of teddy bears…and walking down an aisle that Amanda had strewn with rose petals. I keep asking myself how we got here."

"It was a very sudden, very intense journey," Whitney said gently, "but I think we can make it work."

The searching look Logan gave her made Whitney want to turn and flee. Instead her fingers tightened on the mixing bowl. If only he'd agree with her, if only he'd give her a hint that he believed this was possible, that they could be husband and wife, without two beds, a child and a critical caseworker between them.

"My folks are coming over around eleven," he reminded. "Hey. Your first time with the in-laws."

Whitney tensed, setting the bowl aside. "I can't imagine what I was thinking. I totally forgot about them bringing the wedding gifts over this morning—and after Amanda made such a big deal out of it. I should have thought about fixing a lunch instead. But I can throw a fruit salad together, and I think I saw a muffin mix, and—"

"Whit. They're not coming over to check out how efficient you are in the kitchen."

"I know. But it'll be the first time that we're together."
The strangest light passed through Logan's eyes, as if he
were considering another first. "And I wouldn't want them
to be disappointed. Or thinking I don't appreciate them taking Amanda for the night," she said hastily. "Because they
didn't have to do that, you know."

No, obviously not. The unspoken rejoinder seemed to
bounce off the walls.

"Whitney," Logan said slowly, "I know you're trying
to be a good wife, and you're trying to make sure things
go well, but don't worry about my folks. They'll just take
things at face value anyway."

"But I still ought to serve something, and pick up a little,
before they get here." The last thing Whitney wanted was
for them to discover an unmade bed in the guest room.

"Whatever," he said casually. "But if we're going to
make the most of the firsts, we really ought to start now."
Whitney frowned, unable to discern his meaning as his eyes
slid to her lips. "A morning kiss to start the day. A good
habit to get into. Better than coffee to crank start your engine, and better than pancakes to warm your tummy," he
teased.

The suggestion drew her breath away; she remembered
the kiss they'd shared last night in the foyer. "Are you
making fun of my cooking?" she asked.

"Not at all," he said easily. "I just like your kisses
better than, say, oatmeal."

Whitney raised her head, expecting a friendly peck on
the lips.

Instead Logan paused, and slowly lowered his head, as
if calculating her response. Whitney went weak simply an-
ticipating the moment their lips would touch. At first the
kiss was inquisitive, then he kissed her possessively, his
body melding with hers. His hands tightened around her
waist, her lower back. His mouth inched across hers, yet
when he reached the corner, his lips parted and lifted

slightly. "We really," he whispered, "need to...do this right...especially the first time...as man and wife."

An involuntary sigh escaped Whitney's lungs, and she sagged against him, painfully aware his hands moved as if they had a will of their own, to settle just beneath the curve of her breast. She gave herself fully to the kiss, everything behind her eyelids going blue-black and velvety, just as he pulled away.

"I ought to shower and get cleaned up before everybody arrives," he said huskily, almost apologetically, as his palms slid onto her elbows to ease through the awkward moment of intimacy.

"And I—I've got that fruit salad...."

They pulled apart, both seemingly intent on their responsibilities.

Minutes later, as she opened cans of pineapple and mandarin oranges, Whitney thought about what Logan had said about Walt and Yvonne taking things at face value. More than anything she wanted to convince them that she'd be good for their son, that she could be a mother to Amanda, and part of their family.

Maybe, after Logan dressed, she'd throw a pair of her shoes inside the door of the master bedroom—and a piece of her clothing on the dresser. Just for good looks, and just for good measure.

Walt and Yvonne could only stay until one because after church let out everyone stopped at the marina for supplies. For two hours, however, they were awash in wedding gifts, paper, ribbons and cards.

"Percale pillow slips," Yvonne remarked, fingering the hand-tatted lace and the embroidered hems. "From Aunt Marge. Only she would waste her time, bothering with something like this. I've asked her to work at the marina, but she'd rather stay at home and fiddle with this stuff."

"But they're so beautiful. I'll probably be afraid to use them," Whitney said.

Logan loaded his arms with monogrammed towels and tablecloths. "Yes, and they're going into the linen closet right now, to use, because she'll probably give us another pair at Christmas."

"Logan's right," Yvonne agreed, putting the pillow slips on top of his load. "Here. Let me help you," she offered, following him up the steps with the feather pillows, "and then we've got to go."

Whitney didn't think a thing about their visit until later, when she and Logan were getting ready to take the speed-boat out. Amanda was on the beach, building a most re-markable moat around two wet lumps of sand that was supposed to be a castle. Logan unhooked one of the moor-ing lines and, as he stepped into the boat, slipped an S hook into his pants' pocket. He stopped.

"Whit…?"

"Yes?" She turned to him, ready to hand him the cooler.

"Did you happen to use my shower this morning?"

She frowned. "No…I used the guest bath."

His mouth twitched. "Oh, well, I knew you wanted to pick up this morning, and I thought maybe you were in a hurry and forgot something…" he trailed off, pulling her pink silk panties from his pocket. "I found these. On my dresser."

"Um….oh…" Whitney's mouth worked, but she couldn't bring herself to offer up a logical explanation. See-ing his hands on her favorite pair of underwear was un-nerving.

"If you were looking for them, that is. I didn't know."

She wanted to swipe them out of his hands, but he wouldn't let her, holding them slightly aloft. "I didn't lose them," she hissed finally. "And I wasn't expecting you to find them. I was…trying to make things look real. For your folks."

"Uh-huh." He gave the lingerie a cursory glance, ab-sently rubbing his thumb over the silk. "Well, I'm pleased to announce that your special effects worked. Mom very pointedly suggested that I buy you a lingerie chest for a wedding gift. She tends to like things neat and tidy. She would never leave *her* underwear laying around for just anyone to see.''

Whitney's eyes briefly shuttered closed. ''I didn't mean to embarrass you, Logan.''

He chuckled. ''You didn't. Now tell me, whatever prompted you to think of something like that?''

''It was just one of those impulsive things,'' Whitney answered, refusing to lie.

''That's what I like about you, Whit. You always confess. Even when it hurts.''

''So, okay,'' she admitted, reaching for the panties, ''it hurts. If I yell uncle, will you let me have them—''

He lifted them higher. ''You have a heckuva imagination, lady. I can't wait to see how ingeniously you're going to convince Madeline this marriage is on the up-and-up. I know you'll come up with something good.''

The statement didn't bother her, because she knew Logan was teasing.

''Daddy! Are we ready yet?'' Amanda stood up, impatiently squishing her toes in moat water.

Logan's long fingers gobbled the scrap of pink silk up into the palm of his hand, and before Whitney could protest—or snatch them away—he tucked them safely back into his pocket.

''Logan!''

''We're leaving, pip.'' He glanced down at Whitney, and winked. ''I was just stirring the waters—and trying to make a few waves before we left.''

Whitney, determined not to be outdone, didn't budge. ''Waves, Logan?'' she asked. ''Better be careful. Because you remember that old saying, 'still waters run deep'? You really don't want to get into anything you can't handle.''

He laughed, boldly, as if she'd just extended a challenge.

The following week, they moved Whitney's things in the mornings and camped out at the beach in the afternoons.

Logan had to go back to work by Wednesday, and that same day, after she had arranged for a baby-sitter, Whitney stopped in to check on the shop.

She'd ended up working until midnight, as Donna, her only employee, hadn't been able to put everything aright since the wedding. Donna did confide, however, that she'd be happy to pick up more hours at the shop, so Whitney decided to pare her typical workweek, and take some time to settle in and work around Amanda's summer schedule.

It wasn't a difficult decision to make, for she'd barely put in two hours before she missed her new family. She kept looking at the clock and thinking of all that she was missing. Amanda's snack time, and the chapter she'd promised to read to her. Logan's habit of flipping through all fifty-six channels on the television before settling on the six o'clock news. His small talk while she dawdled making dinner.

So she'd called. Three times. Just to hear their voices, and to say good-night to Amanda…and to tell Logan not to wait up for her, that she'd be late. She thought about him going to bed alone—again—and that was equally troubling.

She wanted to be there to say good-night to him, too. She wanted to hear the hesitancy in his voice as he puttered around the kitchen and made noises about being "really tired." She longed to be there for the curious glances he cast in her direction, solicitously asking if there was anything else she needed.

She imagined the courage it would take to stun him with the reply that was brewing inside her. *Just a drink of water, an extra blanket, a bed partner…like you.*

Whitney sighed heavily, realizing Teddy Bear Heaven was everything to her, but it was a responsibility she could let go—at least for a while, until her new life was on the right track. With a husband and a child, she needed to change her priorities. For, when Logan smiled across the breakfast table at her, or Amanda praised her chocolate chip cookies, cutting back at the shop didn't seem like such a huge sacrifice.

To prove that she could do it, Whitney intentionally took the next two full days off, deciding that the toy show would be her next big outing. They'd already planned it as their quick fix "honeymoon" anyway.

So, at 6:00 a.m. that Saturday morning, a sleepy Amanda stumbled into the kitchen. "Are we ready to go yet?" she asked, yawning around the question.

Whitney bit back a smile as she took in Amanda's bare feet, her wrinkled cotton nightgown and tangled hair. "Good morning," she greeted as she bent down to smooth back her bangs and plant a kiss on the top of her head. "You aren't anxious, are you?"

"Mmm-hmm. I've never been to a toy show before."

"Well, we won't leave for a while. I think your daddy's still asleep, because he worked late last night."

Amanda eyed the toaster pastries framed within the opened cupboard door. "I'll get my own breakfast, if you go wake him up," she bargained. "That would give you less to do."

A shiver skittered down Whitney's spine. She hadn't been in Logan's bedroom yet—at least not while he was in the bed part of it. She let Amanda think they shared the room by keeping her things out of sight in the guest room, and arranging her nighttime hours after Amanda went to bed and before she got up.

"Wait a minute," Whitney protested. "You aren't thinking of toaster pastries, are you? Because I thought you liked my oatmeal."

"It's okay. But like Daddy says, it's second best."

That had already become the family joke: Whitney's oatmeal was second best.

Funny thing was, Amanda didn't realize that it was second best to their morning kisses. Whitney cherished that brief moment of intimacy—and Logan never forgot. Sometimes, when Amanda was around, he'd come up behind her and plant a warm, tantalizing kiss beneath her ear. Other times, he'd kiss her full on the lips.

Yet every time the kiss got just a little heated, Logan would pull back, saying he was late for the office, or he needed to get the truck he'd borrowed back to his dad's dealership, or should go get the car washed. It was always something, and it was always frustrating. Every time they got close, he had somewhere to go, something to do.

It was enough to make a woman wonder how bad her oatmeal was, anyway.

"You better wake him up, Whitney," Amanda prompted. "You said it's a long drive. Remember?"

A squeamish feeling coiled through Whitney. She didn't think she could bear to see Logan's bare shoulders, or his broad chest—because, if she gave him a morning kiss there, in his bed, her imagination would slip her under the covers, beside his bare skin and within his strong arms.

"I've got an idea," she said brightly. "Maybe you can go wake your daddy up."

"No…" Amanda wrinkled her nose, pulled the pastries box out of the cupboard, and trudged to the table. "He'll just figure out a way to horse around in bed, so he won't have to get up."

"Horse around in bed?" Whitney asked unsteadily.

"You know," Amanda answered, concentrating on ripping the individual package carefully from the top. "He acts like he's snoring, or pulls the covers over his head, or wrinkles his nose when you tickle him. You pull the sheets off, he pulls them back on."

"Oh. That." Whitney felt faint, thinking of Logan, with the sheets off.

"Yes," Amanda said decisively, her pink tongue darting out to lick the frosting. "I think you better wake him up."

Some perverse reason made Whitney agree. Maybe it was because she wanted to pull the blinds, and see shafts of light fall across the rugged angles of his body. Maybe it was because she wanted to see if Logan hung one muscular calf over the edge of the bed, or whether he really would pull the covers back if she pulled them off.

Of course, she wouldn't. She'd never dare be that brazen.

Yet, she marched herself up the stairs, then stopped, staring uncertainly at the closed door of the master bedroom. It probably would have been easier to make him an omelet, than chide him about this crazy oatmeal comparison. Besides, she could have used food as an excuse for walking in on him. Food was always a good excuse to avoid what was really troubling you.

Her palm closed around the doorknob, then she hesitated and knocked, lightly, tentatively. She heard a groan.

She knocked again, a little louder. Then she opened the door. "Logan?" she inquired softly, poking her head inside the door. "I'm sorry to wake you. I know it's early." His face was relaxed, unlined, his mouth slack as his eyes lazily opened. "Amanda's up and anxious to go. She wanted me to wake you."

"Mmm," he sighed, then rolled over on his back and pushed the sheet down beneath his arms, exposing his well-sculpted chest and wide shoulders. "Blame her, will you?" His voice was thick, with morning sleep slurring his words. He chuckled, then patted the bed, beside him. "Talk to me a minute. Wake me up."

Whitney eyed the vacant spot at his hip. If she sat there, she'd feel the warmth of his bed on her backside, the heat of his flesh seeping through the sheet. She wasn't sure she wanted to be that close…not yet, not when everything between them was still so uncertain. "I suppose," she said, purposely moving into the room, "that you'd like these blinds opened."

"No. Not particularly."

In spite of herself, and with her back still to him, she smiled. She heard him pat the mattress. She fixed the blinds anyway, tinkering with them. She adjusted one slat that was slightly crooked, then fiddled with the cord, to make sure it was hanging straight. Finally she took a deep breath, and faced the dragon that had been breathing over her shoulder.

But he didn't look like a dragon at all...but a man. Her man. He was heavy-lidded, his cheeks flush with sleep. She ached to smooth his tousled hair into place. Moving to the side of his bed, Whitney forced herself to sit on the edge of it. "I am sorry about barging in here, and waking you—"

He turned on the pillow, then scrinched his eyes against the blinding morning light, and shook his head. "No, I shouldn't have worked so late last night, but I wanted to get the numbers crunched so I didn't have that hanging over my head today. Working around two businesses in the family is going to be a trick, isn't it?"

"Mmm, I know."

"We may want to think this over. I don't want to end up like my folks, always juggling family life around business." He sighed, and absently picked up her hand as he stared at the ceiling. "I realized last night, when it was my turn to burn the midnight oil, that you had a lot of mess in the store to clean up from the wedding, and I had a lot of leftover stuff to take care of from taking so many days off."

"We'll catch up."

"Maybe. But..." He massaged her ring finger, his thumb and forefinger slipping to her wedding ring, straightening it. "You've got this toy show thing this weekend. And I know we'll enjoy it. Still, it's business."

"This time around we're combining business and pleasure. You said."

"Yeah, well...sometimes the business just takes over and you forget it's supposed to be fun."

"How about this?" Whitney suggested, "I promise to never lose track of what's important around here. You do the same."

Logan's eyes narrowed, thoughtfully. "Tell me. What's important?"

Whitney longed to say, "you." But she couldn't bring

herself to reveal that much. Not yet. Not first. "Amanda," she said. "It's important for her that this work out. This home. You..." she said carefully, refusing to elaborate. "I've always wanted a home and family, Logan. But Teddy Bear Heaven is like my home and my baby, too. I can manage both, and Donna's already asked about working extra hours. Just for the summer. Until we know where we're going."

He nodded, slowly, then released her hand. "I guess," he said, "that we just have to think things through. See what the future brings."

He was being deliberately vague, and that distressed her. Rising from the bed, Whitney consciously decided to convince Logan that they could be a family, that they could make it work. "My crystal ball tells me your future has something special in it."

"Oh, and what's that?"

"Me," she said brightly. "And my morning kiss." Leaning down, she took the initiative and kissed him, surprising even herself. He hesitated before kissing her back, but when he did he sent a jolt all the way down to the tips of her toes.

Whitney's knees went weak, and her eyes drifted closed. As she pulled away, she missed the curious, bemused expression on his face.

The toy show was extraordinary. Both Logan and Amanda giggled like conspirators as they tried on the inflatable Sumo wrestler suits. They battled it out with laser swords and handheld video games. They waltzed through the doll collection and experimented with plastic building blocks.

They happily gave Whitney time to browse through the teddy bears and figure out her orders. The only blight on the whole show was that Whitney didn't see anything similar to the teddy Logan had hoped to replace for Amanda.

It was always on her mind. Leaving her with the feeling that if she found it, it could lay to rest some of the past.

"Okay, it's settled," Logan announced, as she turned in her last order for teddy bears, "we know what we want for Christmas, our birthdays and any other gift-giving occasions. We have a list a mile long."

"Mmm? You're planning that far in advance?"

"It's not hard. Amanda wants *everything*. And I've got a few requests myself."

"You've got the best job ever, Whitney," Amanda confirmed. "And I think this is the best honeymoon ever. I'm going to tell everybody all about it."

Logan's mouth twitched; Whitney blushed.

"Even Madeline?" Logan asked.

"Especially Madeline. Because she said it wouldn't be a real honeymoon if I went along—that I'd just be in the way."

Both adults turned to her.

"She said that?" Whitney asked, appalled that Madeline would suggest such a thing to Amanda. Dropping to one knee, she pulled the child into her arms, thinking of how her mother had always referred to her as "a nuisance, and not worth the trouble you're worth." "Amanda," she said earnestly, "don't you believe it. Not a word of it. It wouldn't be the same if you weren't here with us. Both your daddy and I need you."

Logan's hand cupped Amanda's thin shoulder. "It's true, pip. One of the reasons we did this, was because of you."

"The toy show?"

"Well…yeah. That, too."

To both adults the implications were clear.

"You mean, if it weren't for me, you'd have rather done something else for a honeymoon?"

Logan noisily cleared his throat, and stared at the toe of his shoe, as if it were the most fascinating thing on the trade show floor.

Whitney jumped in, rescuing the moment. "What he

means is…that this was a great opportunity to do something we could all enjoy. That's what honeymoons are about, Amanda. Being together. Making memories. Right, Logan?'' Whitney expected Logan to agree immediately, but his expression was unreadable, and the faraway look in his dark eyes made her realize he was thinking of something else entirely.

''Amanda,'' he said slowly, ''Whitney's got it all figured out. Listen to her. She's one smart woman.''

''Well, if you guys want to do something without me, it's okay,'' Amanda assured. ''I could just ride those little trucks for a while. So, if you wanted to fool around with those battery operated toys, or something—just so you could tell Madeline I wasn't always in the way…and you had fun together and everything….''

''We are having fun together,'' Logan assured, ''as a family.''

Whitney offered Logan a sideways glance, and an inexplicable feeling of sadness engulfed her. She didn't regret that their honeymoon included Amanda, her only regret was that their in-name-only marriage didn't include any of the intimacy she craved.

Chapter Twelve

Whitney was a nervous wreck. Three weeks after their hasty marriage she was making her first appearance as Logan's wife and Amanda's mom. Whitney knew full well she'd be under scrutiny, and she wasn't sure she was up to the task. Things had been going well, exceedingly well—until yesterday.

Madeline had made another routine visit and it had left Whitney shaken. Although they'd chatted easily about everyday things, Madeline had lulled Whitney, making her so comfortable that she actually forgot the woman was there to judge her, to see if she'd make an adequate mother, one worthy of parenting six-year-old Amanda.

Whitney had committed the ultimate blunder—she'd confided that Amanda had had a bad dream. While Whitney didn't think it was anything significant, Madeline zeroed in on it. She speculated that maybe Amanda was experiencing a difficult adjustment to their recent marriage, that maybe she felt rejected, or her fear of abandonment had resurfaced. Whitney nearly wilted, valiantly assuring Madeline she didn't think it was anything but a bad dream. Children had bad dreams.

Madeline had simply clucked her tongue and narrowed her gaze at Logan, as if to say, "I told you so."

Afterward, Logan privately commented, "Some things are better left unsaid, especially when the caseworker's here."

Whitney felt like she'd failed the first critical test, and now she had to redeem herself at the ballet recital. She needed to prove to Logan and Amanda—maybe even to herself—that she was the best possible person for this role as wife and mother.

She'd come home early from Teddy Bear Heaven, made sure the house was spotless, the pot roast fork tender and Amanda's costume perfectly pressed. She knew she was overcompensating, but she felt equally compelled to do it. She'd even taken time to French braid Amanda's hair, weaving pink satin ribbons in the plaits.

Yet the moment they arrived at Miss Timlin's dance studio, apprehension gnawed at Whitney, making her stumble the moment she crossed the threshold.

Logan's hand went to her elbow. "You okay?" he asked. "You're white as a sheet."

"I'm just a little nervous," she admitted. "Vicarious stage fright. Amanda's been bubbling on about this for so long. I'm worried...I want it to go well."

He shook his head. "I don't think it's that at all. You're working too hard. We could have grabbed something from the deli tonight, it wouldn't have hurt."

"I just wanted to make sure it—" Whitney deleted "lasts" from her reply "—was something special. For tonight. I feel like it's my first night out in Melville, as a wife and mom."

"Ah...." Comprehension lit his dark eyes. Amanda had skipped ahead of them to the dressing room behind the stage. "I'll do everything I can to make this as painless as possible, Whit. You'll be fine." He grinned down at her, escorting her into the roomful of people as if she was a queen.

The recital itself was delightful, and Whitney was reluctant to see it end.

"Can I get you some punch?" Logan asked afterward, rising.

"Thank you, that would be nice," Whitney followed him as the ballet students, still in costume, streamed down the aisles.

Amanda rushed headlong into Logan's legs, giving him a bear hug. "How was I?" she asked.

"Wonderful," he confirmed. Amanda looked around him, expecting the same response from Whitney.

She nodded. "It was the best recital ever. I'm so proud of you."

At the praise, Amanda flung herself into Whitney's arms. "Thanks. I wanted you to say that." She snuggled against Whitney's neck. "I love you, Whitney. And thanks for making my hair pretty."

The declaration reduced Whitney to putty. She hugged Amanda fiercely, "Love you, too," she whispered against her ear. She looked beseechingly up at Logan, knowing her eyes were watery, her mouth tremulous.

He stepped back, inclining his head, his lips a firm line. "Hey, I'll…um…I'll get that punch for you now."

As Whitney struggled to compose herself, feeling somewhat deserted by Logan, a tall brunette approached.

"Hi, Mrs. Thomas," Amanda said, pulling away. "This is my new mommy."

"Hello," the woman extended her hand, and Whitney had no choice but to straighten and take it. "I'm Carrie's mom, Joyce Thomas. I know you're new, but I thought we might corner you into joining the mothers' booster group. We do things to raise money for the dance troupe…and we have a little fun while we're doing it."

"Oh, it sounds…"

"Wonderful, Joyce," Logan finished, putting the cup of

punch into Whitney's hands. "Just what we need to do, impress my new bride into service. Make her commit to family obligations as soon as it is humanly possible."

Though they all laughed at his wry comments, Logan was secretly pleased. Whitney was everything he could have wanted in a wife. He felt an overwhelming desire to ingrain her in their small family, to tie her irrevocably to them. He found himself wanting to tell her how much he appreciated the way she read to Amanda each night, or how he felt when he saw the single wildflower she placed on the breakfast table each morning. She had won Amanda's heart—and she was steadily chipping away at his.

"I'll look forward to seeing you at the next meeting then, Whitney," Joyce said. "Maybe we can get you on the board or something. Get you involved right away."

"Hey," Logan objected, "don't get too carried away. Newlyweds need a little time together." Joyce laughed, but Whitney looked down, as if she were slightly embarrassed. Logan hung an arm loosely, yet possessively around Whitney's waist and they meandered through the throng of parents and grandparents. Finally Logan whispered, "It's getting late. We need to be going, don't you think?"

Whitney nodded, and allowed him to guide her through the dissolving crowd. On the way home, Amanda hummed in the back seat, her personal CD playing the theme music from the evening's recital. Her toe kicked the back of the seat, keeping time, and the feathers were still in her braided hair. Logan and Whitney exchanged glances, biting back smiles.

"It was a shame your folks couldn't get away for tonight," Whitney said finally.

"You didn't really expect them to, did you?"

"Well, I'm sure they never would have chosen to miss this. Not intentionally."

Logan settled back against the leather seat, as if he were uncomfortable. He glanced up at into the rearview mirror and adjusted it, making sure that Amanda was still listening to her CD player and couldn't hear their conversation. "No. Maybe not intentionally. But...I don't think you really understand my folks, Whit." His right hand moved to the top of the steering wheel, and he experimentally turned it, as if he were interested in the car's response. "Do you remember," he said thoughtfully, "how you always teased me in chemistry about football, saying if I loved my homework as much as I loved that old leather pigskin, I could get those scholar-athlete awards, hands down?"

"Yes?"

"I was a fraud." In the fading light, he recognized Whitney's confusion. "I never even liked football, but I had an ulterior motive for playing it." He let a second of silence slip away. "It got my folks to the game. Having them close up shop and come to see me play meant the world to me. I always felt like I just sort of grew up between two businessmen and a business. I," he said dramatically, "was the by-product of a merger."

"Oh, Logan, no...your folks do care about you." Without realizing it, Whitney mimicked his pose, also sinking back into the leather seats. "I mean...at least they stuck around. My mom never did. She left me at Gram's when I was eight and just took off. I used to want parents so bad that I'd lay awake at nights and make wishes on falling stars. I'd fantasize, maybe my mom would come home, changed, with the dad I'd never met. And then I'd worry that would actually happen, and she'd take me away—to some crazy place like Tasmania." He laughed. "Well, it could have happened, the Tasmanian thing. Knowing my mom."

"She was a character, huh?"

"Was, and still is, I suppose. Doesn't matter. I haven't heard from her in years." Whitney fiddled with a loose button on her jacket and reminisced about her grandmother. "My gram was wonderful. I used to wonder how she could have raised someone like my mom. It didn't seem to fit. Gram was everything Mom wasn't. Kind, caring. I know I had to be a burden to her, but she never complained, not once, about me being in the way.''

"Whitney, your gram was a gem. You two complemented each other. Maybe she was grateful for the way it worked out with you. She probably had her own regrets, if her own daughter…'' He left the rest unsaid.

They idly turned their attention to a group of young boys who were happily skateboarding near the street.

A block later, Whitney asked rhetorically, "Which do you suppose is worse, Logan? Being abandoned by your parents emotionally or physically?''

He shrugged. "I don't know. I used to wish my folks would get their noses out of their bank statements long enough to talk to me.''

Whitney snorted. "I remember this one time my mom called me…to wish me a happy birthday. But she didn't know she'd called five days late. So my gram, she assures me the only reason my mom didn't realize what day my birthday was, was because of the time zone change, that it made a difference with the phone calls.'' Logan laughed, sympathetically. "I *believed* her. Of course, I was only ten. The thing was, I was so shocked that my mom still knew the phone number. I thought she'd forgot where she left me.''

"Both of us should have had hotlines to our parents.''

"I'd have only had one thing to say—be there for me.''

Logan shifted slightly on the seat, his head swiveling in her direction as he switched hands on the steering wheel. Reaching across the console, he squeezed her hand.

"I've always said I wanted to be there for my kids. I mean that. Whatever happens, Logan, I intend to be there for Amanda.''

"I know. I understand. Because if there's one thing I want to achieve in my lifetime, it's putting my family first.''

Whitney hesitated, allowing her hand to be swallowed

up by Logan's as she mustered her courage. "You think I can be part of that family?" she asked boldly.

"I think..." he said, "that, together, we're making a heckuva stab at fixing things that went wrong. This time around, I'm the dad, you're the mom and we got us a little girl in the back seat. From all indications, it looks like family to me. Either that, or we're just playing house."

It wasn't quite the answer that Whitney wanted to hear...especially when she considered that, with them continuing to go to their separate rooms each night, maybe they *were* just playing house. She didn't know if she could bear to see that go on indefinitely.

Logan stared at the pineapple upside-down cake cooling on the counter. She was doing it again. Driving him crazy. Without even intending to. Without even knowing she was doing it.

All the little things were adding up—and just as quickly wearing him down. He'd tried to ignore the potpourri in the foyer, and the floral arrangement in the upstairs hall. But then she'd put scented hand lotion beside the kitchen sink and, every night after they finished the dishes, he'd become absolutely mesmerized by the way she rubbed the lotion between her palms and through her fingers. It had become like a ritual, this watching her.

Then she started tacking pictures of the three of them—the ones where they'd been lazing around on the beach, and playing at the toy show—on the fridge. It seemed no matter where he looked, Whitney was always there, smiling back at him.

It was unnerving. It was unjust. It was unreal.

Whitney was slowly putting her signature on his life, and he couldn't stop it from happening. What was more unsettling was that he didn't know if he wanted to.

When Whitney lit the candles last night for dinner, he could barely eat—all he could see were her luminescent eyes bathed in candlelight. The way her mouth curved when she and Amanda exchanged knock-knock jokes. The coquettish way she'd dab the corner of her mouth with the napkin, and wink at him, then reel off another joke. He kept thinking about jumping over the table and ravishing her, this beautiful, gorgeous creature who was his wife.

He'd played the hands-off game long enough. It was driving him crazy; he wanted to kiss her, and touch her, and take her to his bed. He wanted to know what it felt like in the morning to have her head on his shoulder. He wanted to see her stretch, felinelike, after they were intimate. He wanted to hear her sigh after she was satiated from their lovemaking.

Lovemaking. That was the disturbing crux of it.

It was getting so he couldn't get her out of his head, almost as if he were falling in love with her. And that was what was so unreasonable. He'd said from the beginning that love had nothing to do with it. It was an arrangement, pure and simple.

Yet, inside, it was as if his heart was growing and changing. As if she was moving into his heart, and camping out there, waiting for his head, and all his fuzzy emotions, to wake up and clear.

Sure, he'd fought the occasional surges of guilt that fried his brain and left him weak when he looked at Whitney. That was the bottom line—he felt he was betraying his late wife. When they were married, he'd never once looked at another woman…but now, he simply felt torn—as if he were living in limbo, and aching to crawl out and into the paradise only Whitney could offer.

Come on. How the hell could he think straight and talk logically when he had Whitney Bloom and a pineapple upside-down cake looking him in the eye?

"I'm sorry," Whitney said breathlessly from the doorway. She was wearing those cute little sweats and that baggy sweatshirt again; Logan felt a distinct hitch in his groin. "I was doing laundry, but I thought I heard you call me."

"I did. Until this pineapple thing caught my attention."

Whitney's face fell. "Oh. You don't like pineapple up-side-down cake?"

"Whitney, I love it…but…this has got to stop. Because this way of getting to a man's heart through his stomach is—" dammit, why'd he have to say that? "—working. It's working me out of my clothes." Omigod, it just kept getting worse. "Working me into workouts."

She laughed, that tinkly little sound he'd come to appreciate. "Quit teasing. I almost believed you."

"I honestly came in here to talk seriously about your condo, but that thing distracted me."

"My condo? What about my condo?"

"I heard through the grapevine that Meltech is expanding their operation. Housing is at a premium in Melville. This would be an opportune time for you to sell, so I did an appraisal. Thought you might want to take a look at it, see what you think." He laid the paperwork on the counter, beside that blasted cake.

"Oh, I…" she shrugged, her nose wrinkling. "I can look at it later. I'm really not in any hurry to—"

"Whit, these people are transient. This could be a golden opportunity for you to cash in."

"Logan, I promise you, when I'm ready to get rid of the condo, you'll be the first to know." She turned away to fold a towel that was lying on the table.

"Well, I spent all afternoon doing this market analysis for you. I thought—"

"It's not like we have to sell it, is it?"

"Well, no…"

"I just don't want to. Not yet. Sometimes I stop over there for lunch. And I don't have everything cleaned up and decorated the way it should be. It could probably stand a coat of paint. And the caulk around the sink needs to be done."

Excuses. She was offering him up a dozen lame excuses. It occurred to him that maybe she wasn't ready to let go of the condo because she was having second thoughts about this "in name only" marriage. Maybe she *really* was just doing him a favor—and she'd walk after the adoption was final. A horrible sense of foreboding filled him.

His imagination simply couldn't stretch that far. A world without Whitney in it?

"You can…look at it. If you want," he said flatly. "It's up to you, I guess."

Whitney hadn't been able to think straight—the closest she and Logan had come to exchanging words, particularly harsh words, were over the condo. She knew the condo was costing her money, that it would be the logical thing to do, to sell it. Yet every time she thought about this marriage failing, about losing Amanda—and Logan—she knew she had to have a safe place, a retreat.

What if she got everything just the way she wanted it— her child, her husband and her home—and it fell apart? It would be her undoing. It would destroy her. She needed that condo, if for no other reason than that it was her own private security blanket.

She simply couldn't bear the thought of starting all over again. Familiar surroundings would be her only saving grace, and yet…she'd trade the condo in a moment if it would only solidify her place with Logan.

She had to face facts: she was more in love with Logan than when she'd started this little fiasco. She was so much in love her heart hurt.

She was still in a quandary over the condo issue when Madeline came into the shop three days later.

"Whitney. Hi! I was in the neighborhood and thought I'd drop in. I can call this an official visit, if you've got a moment."

"Sure, that would be fine." Whitney warily pushed

shredded paper packing back into the box and pushed it aside, waiting for Madeline to go on.

"Amanda was positively stunning at the recital. Her hair was so cute."

"You were there?" So, Madeline *was* spying on them.

"Only for a short time. I'd intended to say hello, but you looked like you were busy and I needed to get home, so…" Madeline left the explanation hang. "All in all, it appears Amanda's doing fine. I saw all I needed to see."

"She is. I enjoy her so much that sometimes I just can't imagine what my life used to be like without her."

"A lot better than going home alone to that condo, huh?"

"Really." Whitney paused, reflecting on all the joy Logan and Amanda had brought into her life. "I never thought things could be so good."

"Say…about that condo…." Madeline's eyes were sharp, piercing. "I was out that way, and noticed you hadn't put it on the market yet."

"Well, I…" Whitney took a deep breath, wondering if she could manage a decent explanation. "I guess it hasn't been on our list of priorities. Though Logan did mention something to me about it the other day."

"He did?"

"I think he wants the listing," Whitney said conspiratorially, embellishing the statement with a wink. "But I want to do some painting, things like that. It would cut me to the quick to have him list it as a fixer-upper."

Madeline laughed. "Well, I just thought I'd check… because I was ready to push this adoption through, and then I noticed that, and…I wondered what was going on. Or if maybe your life, with the move and the marriage and all, is too hectic right now. Especially to deal with these adoption issues."

Whitney's heart hammered, her hands trembled and her vision blurred. She couldn't afford to lose everything over the sale of one condo. It was just a place to sleep, and little else. "No, no. It's a good time. A very good time. Logan and Amanda come before anything else. And maybe that's why the condo has been lingering like it has. It just..," she took a deep, cleansing breath, "isn't important to me anymore."

"Whitney? I don't think you'll be sorry. Not on any of this." To her surprise, Madeline reached over the narrow counter and patted her arm before leaving.

Whitney was shaking when she dialed Logan's office. His secretary, who now recognized her voice, said he was busy. Whitney asked her to interrupt him. He was on the line immediately.

"Whit? What's up?"

"I need to talk to you." She tried to force a calm she didn't feel into her voice. "About the condo? I want to get the listing written immediately. If you want, you can put a For Sale sign in the yard today."

For a moment there was nothing but the hum of dead silence over the wires. "Why the sudden change of heart, Whit?"

"Call it a revelation. I just need to get it out of the way, instead of postponing the inevitable." She hesitated. "It is inevitable, isn't it, Logan?" She vaguely wondered if he could hear the innuendo, if he understood what she was really asking.

"Yeah, Whit. I think it is."

Chapter Thirteen

Logan studied the form, making sure he hadn't omitted anything. He'd probably filled out hundreds of listings, but this time around it was different, personal. Whitney's reluctance deeply disturbed him. "You know, Whit, we can wait if this doesn't feel right to you."

"No. We have to do it," she said firmly, not looking at him as she ran a wet finger over the caulk she'd put around the sink while he'd measured the rooms.

"C'mon. Give me a little latitude here. I mention it to you and you put me off, and we nearly fight about it. Then a week later, you're hell-bent on selling. Something isn't adding up."

Whitney cleaned off the tip of the caulk. "I had time to think about it, that's all. I realized it would be better for all of us if we just go ahead, as planned."

"Hey. Look at me." He braced against the breakfast bar, putting himself at a spot where she had to look at him. "You have any objections about sharing my home? We moved you in rather quickly, I know, but at the time—"

"It made sense," she finished for him.

They were starting to do that, finishing sentences for each other, thinking each other's thoughts. It was a marriage thing, and the intimacy of it, especially with Whit, astonished him. "Look, if you're not comfortable—"

"How could I not be comfortable, Logan? You have everything. Five bedrooms, three baths, a library and a gourmet kitchen. A private beach and a bunch of toys that run on water."

"Well, there are other degrees of comfort," he said, rocking back on his heels. "Emotional comfort. Physical comfort." She didn't even blink, as if she didn't have the slightest idea what he was talking about. "Maybe we should think about a different place. For both of us."

Whitney considered this as she capped the caulk and set it back, behind the faucet. "Not necessary, Logan. I'm not trying to be a martyr about this, my only concern is Amanda's welfare. Really."

He stared at her, unconvinced. Sure, he could move her into his home, but how was he going to move her into his heart? Most of the time it still felt as if his head and heart were moving in different directions—and he had no clue at all what hers were doing. "Maybe," he said, draping his forearm over her shoulder, and moving closer over the counter, "if we stay there, in my house, we should think about redecorating."

Whitney curiously tilted her head. "Why?"

"Well...they aren't your things," he said awkwardly, trying to smooth over the fact that she'd inherited all of his first wife's choices. "But I've liked all the little things you've done around the house, the potpourri, the candles, the teddy bears in the den. Maybe, together, we could do more. Make it *ours*," he emphasized, his forehead only inches from hers. "Like the master bedroom," he suggested, "it could really use an update."

Whitney stared at him, blankly. "I don't know," she said evasively. "Besides, we agreed we'd take our time."

Logan felt another surge of helplessness coming on. He

had this overwhelming need to make things right by her, and she wasn't cooperating. *Take their time?* Yeah, they agreed to take their time—about everything—and all it was doing was taking him to the loony bin and back.

Hearing a crash upstairs, and the dead silence that followed, Logan rushed to investigate. He took the steps two at a time, fearing Whitney might have fallen in the shower.

"Amanda! Be careful," he heard her admonish. "What are you trying to do? Break all the drawers?"

"No. They're steps, so I can get up to the top, and put these necklaces away."

Logan paused on the landing, relief whooshing from his lungs. He listened as beads *chirred* against each other, dropping into the velvet-lined drawer.

"Here…let me help you before you fall."

"I'm okay."

"Mmm. But your mother's jewelry armoire may not be."

"I was just playing," Amanda said defensively. "I didn't mean to break it."

"I know. But…" The distinctive sound of a drawer closing interrupted Whitney's reply. "Your mother had beautiful jewelry, honey. Someday her jewelry box will be yours, and I guarantee you won't want it scratched and all banged up."

"Well, I couldn't reach." Over Amanda's distinctive whine, Logan heard the mirrored top drop into place. "You're not mad at me, are you, Whitney?"

Whitney chuckled, as if she couldn't help herself. "No, I'm not mad at you. I'm sorry if you thought I was. Seeing you like that, playing with your first mom's jewelry, it just reminded me of myself, that's all." More drawers closed and opened. "Come on. Let's take this whole drawer of bracelets over to the bed and I'll tell you a story."

Logan slumped against the wall, imagining both Whitney and Amanda sprawled out on his bed, talking.

"When I was about your age, maybe a little older, my mom had to leave, so she gave me to my grandmother to take care of."

"Your real mom gave you away?" Amanda asked, awed. "Like me? Like my real mom gave me away?"

"Sort of. But I was a lot older than you when it happened." Bracelets jingled, hitting against each other. "At first, I missed my mom a lot. And I worried what was going to happen to me."

"You know," Amanda confided, "sometimes I do, too."

"Mmm. I understand that feeling, kiddo," Whitney said. "But your daddy's a lot like my gram. He wouldn't let anyone take you away, not for anything. Anyway, I talked to Madeline a few days ago, and it looks like this adoption is going to be a done deal. You're getting your daddy and me, whether you want us or not."

"Really? For sure?"

"Yep."

"I want you, Whitney. I want you a lot. You and my dad are great."

Logan's eyes shuttered closed, and he considered creeping down the steps before he was discovered eavesdropping. He took the first step away, then heard Whitney say, "You know, my mom never wrote or called. At least not very often. But she'd send me this really awful jewelry."

Amanda giggled.

"She did! I'm not kidding. She sent me this terrible giraffe pin once, with green painted eyes and I just hated it." Amanda said something Logan couldn't make out. "My gram made me wear it to school, and all the kids made fun of it. I wanted to throw it away, but I didn't—and that made me stronger. I'd look at all the other kids who had moms to go home to, and whenever anyone would say something, I'd just look them in the eye and say my mom sent that giraffe to me from South Africa. I made it sound like it was the most important thing in the world...and in a way it was. Because it reminded me of my mom, and it kept her memory close.''

"You don't wear dumb jewelry anymore, Whitney."

"No. Because I grew up and realized I don't have to wear it, not in order to remind myself how much I loved my mom. I know I still love her, no matter what. But what's happened is in the past. It's put away. Like a memory. I still have her jewelry, and sometimes I take it out and look at it, and remind myself how much my life has changed...and how she's still the same. You know, I haven't seen my mom in years and years.''

"Is that why you wanted another family, like us?"

Whitney made a choking sound that Logan imagined was supposed to be a laugh. "Yes, that's exactly it. That's exactly why I wanted another family, a family where I could love someone and they could love me back.''

"I'll always love you, Whitney.''

"The feeling's mutual, kiddo.''

It would have been a lot easier just to creep down the stairs and off into the sunset, but Logan couldn't bring himself to do it. He thought of Whitney and all the sacrifices she'd made for him, and for Amanda. She really hadn't asked for much, just to be loved. Like anyone, that's all she'd ever really wanted out of life.

A guilt so deep, so profound, pervaded his soul. He hadn't done enough for her, he hadn't told her how much he appreciated all she'd done, all she'd committed herself to. If he was going to do it, now was the time. Energy that he hadn't had in months, flowed through his body, suffusing his system and propelling him forward and into his own bedroom. He wanted to say something tender and kind... but he wasn't prepared for the vision Whitney made as she draped herself across his bed with Amanda cuddled against her.

"I..." The word died on his lips. "I...thought I heard something fall.''

Whitney, who was on her side and propped up on one

elbow, turned. Save for a raspberry-red towel that was
tucked in at the top of her breasts, she wore nothing else.
Her shoulders curved, her elbows creased. Gold and silver
bracelets danced on her wrists. Slim bare legs tapered down
into dainty ankles—and toes that Amanda had just last
night painted red, wiggled.

Oh, brother.

She straightened, and tried to sit up, and the towel pulled
apart, exposing the inside of a creamy-white thigh.

Logan sucked in a ragged breath. He wanted her so much
his vision was crossed and his thinking was addled.

"It was just a drawer," she explained hastily, pulling at
the bracelets on her wrists, as if she expected to be flogged
for trying them on. "I fixed everything, and—"

"It's okay," he said. "Like you said, it's just a drawer."

"Well, I didn't want you to think I was…" The bangle
bracelet stuck, and she desperately yanked at it.

"Whit…." Logan moved to the bed like he was on autopilot. Sinking a knee onto the mattress, he joined his wife
and daughter. "You're gonna hurt yourself, doing that.
Here." Taking the fine bones of her wrist between his fingers, he eased the gold circle back, then over the joint of
her thumb. He stroked the flesh on the back of her hand.
"You've got all these red marks…."

"Well, I shouldn't have—" She tried to sit even
straighter and the towel pulled, loosening the knot at her
breasts. She slapped a palm against it, and the bracelets on
her opposite wrist tinkled together.

"Did you and Whitney have a nice chat, pip?" Logan
asked Amanda.

"We sure did!" Amanda beamed.

Logan's mouth twitched, and he knew at that very moment that he had to keep Whitney in his life. He loved her
discomfiture. He loved the way she sat, wrapped in a towel,
and all sprawled on his bed, playing with jewelry and talking to his daughter like they were best friends at a slumber
party. He loved her cleverness and her resilience. He loved

her kindness and compassion. He loved her witty remarks and unbridled imagination.

Could he possibly be falling *in love* with her?

Hearing Logan's key in the lock, that evening when he returned from the office, Whitney looked up from the page she was reading. Amanda was so enthralled with the story, she didn't even move.

He peeked around the corner, the most peculiar expression on his face. "All ready for bed, pip?"

From beneath the hem of her nightgown, she wiggled her bare toes. "I took my bath and everything. Can't Whitney read the next chapter?"

He smiled. "Nope. Whitney and I are discussing the next chapter."

Amanda looked at him. "What? You haven't even read this story."

"No, but it's twenty minutes past your bedtime." Amanda groaned, knowing full well the jig was up. "We're going to paint the playhouse tomorrow," he reminded. "And you have to help."

"Okay, all right already," Amanda said, kissing Whitney's cheek and sliding off her lap to give her dad a hug and a kiss. "You going to tuck me in?"

"I can."

Amanda scurried past Logan and trotted up the stairs. He followed her, thinking how easy this family routine had become. She stopped at the bathroom to brush her teeth, and he hauled stuffed animals off her bed in order to turn down her comforter. He had barely plumped the pillow when she hopped in and pulled the covers up.

"You have a good sleep, pip."

"Thanks, Daddy."

"I love you."

"I love you, too."

The lilt in her voice warmed his heart. He kissed the tip of her nose and started to rise.

"Daddy?"

"Yes?"

"Whitney yelled at me today."

Logan paused, then sat back down, momentarily confused. "You mean...about the jewelry box?"

"Yes. But I wanted you to know she didn't sound at all like Kelly's dad when he yells."

"I'm relieved to hear that."

"I know. She was worried I'd hurt myself, or break the jewelry box. That's why she yelled like that."

"Well, how about that?" He leaned back, trying to fashion a bemused expression on his face. "I guess that just goes to show how much Whitney cares about you."

Amanda turned her head on the pillow, her voice dropping to a confidential stage whisper. "You know what I think about Whitney?"

"No? What?"

"She's the best."

A chuckle rattled in the back of his throat.

"And she can tell the best stories," Amanda praised. "I don't know why she bothers to read them, not when she can tell them like that."

His smile widened. "Should I tell her you approve?"

"No. I'll tell her myself. Someday."

"Someday? Why are you waiting?"

"Because I'm collecting all the things that are different about her that I like."

Twining his finger around a loose thread from the comforter, Logan frowned. "You lost me," he said slowly. "You're collecting what?"

"Daddy, don't you remember? You said she was different. From Mommy. So I started collecting all the things that were different about her. Just to see if she could be just as different and just as good. At the same time."

"Really?" He grew curious. "Could you think of something different? To tell me?"

Amanda nodded. "Well, I think of it like this...Mommy let me lick the egg beater, but Whitney lets me lick the spoon."

Logan lifted both eyebrows. "Now that's an interesting observation."

"And Mommy rolled my socks together, but Whitney folds them in half."

Logan's eyes twinkled. "So even though it's different, it's the same, and you still end up having two clean socks. Right?"

"Right." Crossing her arms atop the comforter, she looked up at him. "And Mommy put sugar on her grapefruit, but Whitney uses salt."

"I didn't know that."

"Well, she does. So you know what? I tried both ways...and I found out I liked grapefruit just as much with salt as with sugar. Isn't that something?"

He patted her hands and winked, his smile growing. "It sure is."

"She laughs just as much as Mommy did, too. And you know why I think she laughs so much?" He shook his head. "Because she likes you."

A hard lump of emotion suddenly caught in his windpipe, taking his breath away. It wouldn't go up and it wouldn't go down. Logan didn't quite know what to say, not to his child.

"You were right, Daddy," Amanda went on. "Whitney isn't trying to take Mommy's place, and I can love her, just because she's her. I'm so glad you found Whitney again, Daddy."

While Logan and Amanda were upstairs, going through her nighttime ritual of teeth brushing and face washing, Whitney put the book away and picked up a few stray building blocks, then propped Amanda's favorite doll in the wing chair.

"You're still working?" Logan asked, coming back into the room a few minutes later.

"Not working, exactly." She picked up a drinking glass to carry to the kitchen.

He took it out of her hand, and put it back on the chair-side table. "Do it tomorrow," he suggested. "A little clutter is good for the soul."

"Now that is original. About as good as you and me discussing the next chapter."

"Actually...there was something I wanted to talk about. Come upstairs. I want you to see this." He didn't wait for her response, but went right back up the adjacent staircase, automatically turning into the master bedroom.

Whitney followed, but stopped to look down the hall, to make sure Amanda's door was cracked open. She liked just a little light in her room before she went to sleep.

Whitney stopped short, just over the threshold of his bedroom, noticing an empty spot in the room. The large jewelry armoire had been removed. She vaguely wondered how Logan had moved it without her hearing, and what he'd done with it.

"I got you something," Logan said softly. He stood off to the side, and quietly closed the door behind her, indicating he didn't want to wake Amanda.

"You're kidding, right?"

"Nope. Not at all. Junk jewelry, so you'll keep me close to your heart."

Whitney's jaw slid off center, and she swiveled on her heel, to face him. During the moment of uncomfortable silence, she wondered if he was poking fun at her.

"I couldn't help hearing what you said to Amanda today. But it wasn't like I was eavesdropping or anything. I heard the crash, and came up to see what was going on, to make sure you hadn't fallen through the shower door." He paused, sliding a look over her. "I was pretty impressed, Whitney. The things you said to her, the way you accepted what she had to say."

She waved off the praise. "It was just the moment, Logan. A spontaneous thing."

"Even so, when I came in here and saw you on the bed...with bracelets up to your elbows—"

She held a hand up, stopping him. "Logan, I'm sorry. I had no right. They weren't mine, and I know I shouldn't have been pawing through them like—"

"Hold on, will you?" He snorted, shaking his head. "I had this great speech prepared, and you're not letting me say it."

"A speech?"

"Yeah. About how perfect you looked there. With Amanda, on my bed, talking, with this towel barely covering your—" She winced; he cleared his throat. "Um, maybe I better start again, and delete that part." He pulled in a deep, cleansing breath. "Okay. I want you to know, Whit, I don't care about the jewelry, or you trying it on. But I thought, afterward, about what you said about the junk jewelry, and how you looked with that tennis bracelet swinging from your fingers." He tossed a long, slim box on the center of the bed. "I thought maybe you should have—or deserved, I don't know—something of your own. So I'm confessing. I didn't go over to my folks tonight, I went to the mall."

Whitney's mouth went dry, and her shoulders sagged. "Oh, Logan." She stared at the box, unable to move.

"Go ahead. Open it."

She moved stiffly, pausing at the foot of the bed, then going knee-down on the mattress, to reach for it. She sat, the backs of her legs hanging over the edge. The mattress shifted slightly as Logan moved to sit beside her.

"I don't know why I wanted to give it to you here. Maybe to recreate the moment, either that, or to change and adjust it," he said softly. "To make it yours."

A lump as big as the state of Texas moved into Whitney's throat. She didn't want to go all sappy on him, and blinked furiously, trying to clear her vision. "Junk jewelry

doesn't come in blue velvet boxes,'' she finally managed
to say. ''It comes on dry as dust cardboard, or wrapped in
plastic, with little foil stickers that say Made In Japan.''

''Mmm. Well, maybe this isn't that exotic then.''

Whitney pensively stroked the blue velvet, reluctant to
open the case. ''I've never gotten many presents, so I—I
don't open them quickly. Kind of like savoring the excitement, I suppose—''

Logan's head fell back, his chest rumbling as he chuckled. ''Hell, honey, if you want to think this over, we can
stay here all night.''

Her hand stopped moving over the blue velvet. Her eyes
cleared, and she sobered, nailing him. ''Logan? You've
never said that before.''

''I'm sorry. I don't swear much but—''

''No. No…the honey part.''

''Oh—I…'' He lifted an apologetic shoulder. ''It just
rolled off my tongue. I guess people you care about should
have special names.'' The way she gazed at him, as if she
didn't quite believe him, made his heart wrench. ''I do care
about you, Whit. That's why I got you this, to show you
how much you've affected my life. How much you've affected me.''

''It—it made me feel like a wife. When you called me
that.''

He hesitated. ''Yeah, well, I think maybe that's something we should fix, too…'' he muttered, taking the box
away from her. ''I can't stand the suspense,'' he said needlessly, lifting the lid without ever giving her the opportunity, ''and there's going to be lots more presents in your
life. I'm going to see to it. So get used to it, or you're
going to have to open them a whole lot faster.'' He gave
her a brief glimpse of the sapphire-and-diamond tennis
bracelet, then freed it from the velvet-covered prongs. Lifting it, he carefully slid it over her wrist, clasping it. ''It
matches your rings, see?''

''Oh, Logan,'' she breathed. The gold slithered down her

forearm, the brilliant baguette stones glittering beneath the light from the bedside table. "I've never, ever had anything this beautiful."

"Whitney?"

"Yes?" She absently turned the bracelet on her wrist, silently admiring it.

"There're times I feel like I've never had anything this beautiful, either. I want you to do more than feel like my wife," he said. "I want you to be my wife...in every sense of the word. This afternoon, I saw you all wrapped up in that towel, and I—" his eyes shuttered briefly "—I kept thinking about how much I care for you, and how good we could be together..." Whitney's breathing grew shallow, and she stared at the unfamiliar bracelet on her wrist. "This isn't a bribe, Whit. If you want to say no, if you're not ready, I'd understand. I'd wait until..."

Until what, she ached to ask. *Until you loved me?* And what if that never happened? What if she remained only the woman, the wife in his house, the one that he lived with?

"I believe you," she said too quickly. "And I want to be your wife. In every sense of the word." *I only wish you could love me,* she silently agonized as her arms looped around his shoulders.

His head was against her cheek, and he rained kisses on her neck, making her blood go hot as desire pulsed through her veins. The old familiar tap dance started drumming through her again.

"That damn towel," he muttered against her throat. "That damn, damn towel. I'm going to throw everything else out and insist we only have raspberry-red towels, so every time I see one, I think of you." She laughed, but the sound was hoarse, gutteral. "I mean it, Whit." His hand slipped to the top button on her knit shirt. "I kept thinking how it would be to give that towel a little tug...and you'd lose it...all of it...and you'd give yourself to me...." The button front separated beneath his expert fingers, and he slipped inside, his palm flat against her shuddering breast.

Whitney unwittingly arched.

"Ah, Whit...these past few weeks, living beside you, seeing you every day..." He kissed her full on the mouth, tasting her, teasing her as his fingers slipped beneath the elastic of her bra.

Her breasts went firm, her nipples going hard and round.

Everything felt tight, constrictive. She needed to be out of these clothes, she needed to feel his flesh against hers. Struggling against him, she tried to shake the shirt away from her shoulders; the movement only aroused him more, and he groaned as he laid her back on the bed.

His hand slid beneath her back, to unfasten her bra, but she stopped him, whispering, "The front. The closure is in the front...."

He found the plastic closure, but toyed with it, his fingers splayed wide to stroke both breasts, coming just short of the peaks. The sensation was agonizing, and he seemed to take pleasure in tormenting her. Over and over, he abraded her skin, arousing her, making her breathing short, erratic. It seemed forever before he stroked the nubile points.

Finally he snapped the closure and the silky material pouffed up, like a mere wisp of frosting that needed to be swiped away. He kissed her throat, and moved down to nudge the frothy undergarment aside. He lapped at the nipple, laving it with his tongue before taking it in his mouth. The pressure he exerted sent waves of heat through her belly, and it spiraled downward, coiling in her loins. Whitney whimpered, involuntarily, and her legs went slack.

He paused.

"Logan...?"

"Oh, baby. You're so beautiful...I just...I just want to make sure this is right," he said thickly, his mouth moving against her flesh. "You're sure you want to do this? Because I want you to stay with me tonight...the whole night...."

In response, Whitney pushed clumsily at the waistband of her slacks, pushing them down as far as the soft part of her belly. He chuckled, and helped her as she changed her tack and gathered his sport shirt, pulling it over his shoulder blades and up under arms. Her hands swirled over his lean back, reveling in the planes and angles that were uniquely Logan.

He cradled her and she instinctively lifted her hips, her slacks falling into a puddle on the floor next to the bed.

Logan shed his shirt, then unbuckled his belt and lifted off of her to step out of his jeans. He was naked when he lay down beside her, and he wasn't hesitant to probe against her thigh, or at the juncture of her legs. He traced the outline of her panties, curiously testing the elastic. He chuckled.

"These the ones you left laying around for my mom?"

"Logan!"

She tried to sound shocked, but he knew she wasn't. "I was hoping they were. For old times' sake."

Her laugh was slight, and sexy as hell. It was all he needed to put his whole hand down inside, to cover the mound of her curls and stroke them before delving into her folds. When she shuddered and arched, his fingertips responded, discovering the source of her moistness, her heat.

Everything inside him started pulsating. His drive to possess her transcended all he'd ever known. He wanted her scent, her touch, her taste. He couldn't get enough, not of everything that made Whitney unique. With her he wanted to soar, he ached to climb to a level of sensuality he'd never before attained.

Her name started echoing through his head, and he vaguely wondered if he uttered it aloud. *Whitney... Whitney...Whitney...* It was so seductive, and as deceptive as a caress, with a mind-bending explosion at the end. It tunneled through his brain, end over end, and somehow, during this torment, he settled between her legs and entered her.

Her curves, as they joined, were supple, pliant. Still, he cradled her shoulders, rocking rhythmically above her. When she writhed, her hair tangled against his cheek, and ground against the hollow of his neck. Relishing every tremor and tremble her body offered up, he stroked her until she was defenseless, and limp. Her legs, bent at the knees, swung heavily against his midsection. Then she arched, from the small of her back, her head going back as if drawn by a silken cord.

"Logan…?" She floundered in his arms, momentarily struggling with the sensations that were pulling her tight. "Logan…?"

Her voice sounded so far away, but he pulled her close against him—and then he felt her snap. From the inside out.

Waves of pleasure circled him, drawing him to his final moment. His body crescendoed, mimicking her ecstasy.

They sank into the mattress together. Fulfilled and drowsy with a new shared joy.

"Logan?"

"Mmm?" He was so weary, so satiated, he could barely lift his head from her shoulder. Still embedded in her, he absently tangled her hair between his fingers, rubbing it as if it were spun gold.

"Maybe I shouldn't say this…"

"No, go ahead," he encouraged. "It's okay."

"When I was married before, it was never like that for me," she said, awed. "It was never this incredible."

He smiled up at her and answered without thinking. "Not for me, either, honey. Not for me, either."

Chapter Fourteen

Madeline called with startling news: she wanted the adoption finalized before Amanda's seventh birthday and had already secured a court date.

"This will really give us something to celebrate," Whitney said happily, as she placed the casserole on the table and sat down to join her family.

Logan grinned and broke a dinner roll in half. "Yes, Mrs. Monroe, it will." He'd been saying that a lot lately. Mrs. Monroe this, Mrs. Monroe that. As if he was as proud as a peacock that he had the privilege of calling her that.

To top it off, Whitney had stumbled onto more good news. This afternoon, she'd located the teddy bear Logan requested when he first came into her shop. She'd noticed a small ad in her *Barely Bears Repeating* magazine. The teddy had been a promotional item from a small, now-defunct, chain store that had briefly operated in Tennessee. The woman had had three cases of leftover bears; Whitney took them all. Every last one.

She wasn't telling anyone, though. Not until they were safely delivered.

"I had some good news of my own today," Logan said smoothly, helping himself to another hefty portion of chicken and rice. "Someone came in the office, specifically asking about your condo."

"Oh?" Suddenly Whitney's enthusiasm waned. Since nothing had happened, and they hadn't had any real lookers, Whitney had dismissed the matter. It was an out of sight, out of mind proposition.

"They loved it, Whitney. They're young, eager to own their own place, they had all kinds of ideas for the living room. Not that much unlike what you'd wanted to do."

Whitney's head bobbed up and down, woodenly, while a feeling of dread pooled in her middle.

"They immediately made an offer," Logan went on, his eyes alight, as if he'd just wangled the toughest deal in real estate to date. "It wasn't what we expected, but I thought about it, and figured we don't really need the money, so—" he shrugged "—why not? I loosely agreed that we could come to terms and accept their offer."

Rice stuck to the roof of Whitney's mouth, the chicken she was chewing went as dry and tasteless as a sunbleached bone. "You sold the condo?" she managed to ask. "Without telling me?"

"Well, unofficially."

"Logan...maybe you don't need the money, but I do."

"It's only a few thousand dollars." Logan picked up a second roll.

"A few thousand dollars to you means something entirely different to me," Whitney stated, unable to keep the edge from her voice. "You should have asked."

Logan frowned. "That's what I do, Whit, sell houses. It was an opportunity that I didn't want to pass up."

Amanda looked up, her worried gaze going from one to the other.

"Never mind. We'll discuss it later," Whitney said, pushing her untouched plate back a fraction of an inch.

"I'm not hungry anymore. Can I go out and play?"

Amanda asked, putting down her chicken leg. Her mouth drooped, and sadness rolled through her eyes.

Whitney felt as guilty as sin for raising her voice. "I've got your favorite dessert," she said. "Chocolate cake, white frosting."

"Could I have it later?"

"I guess. If you want." Whitney watched Amanda hurry out the back door and run to the swing set.

Logan wadded up his paper napkin and threw it over his plate. "Okay. What's up?"

"You can't just sell my condo," Whitney retorted. "Not without consulting me first."

"I am consulting you. Now."

"I can't afford to take much of a loss."

"Whitney, you said it yourself, the place needs work."

"You had no right, Logan. Not to sell it without discussing it with me."

"I'm trying to discuss it with you. The place needs to be repainted, the upstairs carpet needs to be replaced. The kitchen appliances are on their last legs, and the tile in the upstair bath needs to be redone. Whitney, those things take money, and I have to find buyers who are able to look beyond those things."

"I never claimed it was a mansion, Logan."

"Whit! What's gotten into you? It was a good home for you, there was nothing wrong with it. But it could be a hard sell, and it could end up costing you money. I have potential buyers who really want this place, and they are willing to put the time and effort into it."

"The condo's in my name. It wasn't ethical for you to accept their offer."

"Whitney, I'm doing this for you!"

"Boy, does that sound like my first husband. Every time he took something away from me, he claimed it was in my best interest. Every time he withdrew money from my account and made a mess of my bank statement, or ran up the charge cards, it was always supposed to be for me, so

we could have a better life. Only he was the only one ben-
efiting from it. I got stuck with the bills and three jobs to
pay for them.''

"That was then,'' Logan said hotly. "This isn't even
remotely the same.''

"It isn't?'' Whitney snorted. "The last I knew my name
was on that mortgage. I'll be the one taking the loss.''

"It's not that much!''

"You men are all alike. You think you can just waltz in
and take everything away, and make all the decisions.
You're trying to steal my independence, that's what!''

"I'm trying to get rid of an albatross that's hanging
around your neck,'' he growled. "Between that condo and
your memories of what married life is—''

"Don't even go there.'' She hurled the words at him.
"You don't have any idea. No idea at all. I never lived this
little life in the ivory tower, I had to fight and scratch and
work for everything I ever got…but at least I tried to do it
in an honest, respectable manner. Maybe my first husband
was a thief, but I never expected you'd be one, too, Logan
Monroe. I never thought—''

"What?'' He stared at her, incredulously, as if he
couldn't have possibly heard her correctly. He didn't bother
to wait for her response. "I made a verbal commitment,
Whitney, because I felt it was the right decision at the time.
I thought if you wanted to put the condo on the market,
you intended to sell it. I didn't think the issue was money,
and it never, ever occurred to me that by acting as your
agent, to sell the condo, I was somehow taking your independence away. As for being a thief—''

"Forget I said that.''

"It's a little late now.''

Whitney slumped back in her chair and looked outside.
Amanda was swinging on the tire swing Logan had hung
for her last week and it was apparent she'd heard a portion
of their argument. Her sneakers were dragging, toe end first,

in the dirt. She looked so sad and unhappy, Whitney's heart wanted to break.

"As for being a thief, stealing your independence was the last thing on my mind. If you value your independence so much, I'll understand if you feel your commitment to me and Amanda is exhausted. If you don't want—"

"Logan! I—that's not it," she blurted. "You don't understand. That was my home."

His face was rock solid. "I thought this was your home."

"This is…where you live. I just sort of…joined you here. Because, at the time, it made sense."

"Well, right now, not a damn thing makes sense to me. What do you want me to be? An old friend? Or your real estate agent? Your husband, or…hey, maybe you'd rather I went back to being your roommate? Or maybe the marriage is over because I sold your condo, and assumed you'd stay here?"

"Logan, don't!" Whitney's frustration roiled below the surface of her thinly veiled emotions. "Neither of us deserve the things we're saying to each other."

His mouth settled into a fine, hard line. "What do you want to say then? That it looks like I made a mistake—or maybe we made a mistake, and the condo is the least of our worries."

She guessed at his meaning. She'd have to accept things the way they were or bail out. Maybe she couldn't make him love her, but he'd never intentionally hurt her, she knew that. This was his way; he'd be brutally honest, agonizingly straightforward.

One reckless thought surged through Whitney: it was time to admit her fears, to take the chance that he'd understand. "Logan…listen…that condo was the only security I ever had. When things went wrong I could go there and hole up, and assure myself that I was safe, that I'd be okay. So, if anything happens, and this all falls apart, I don't know where I'll go if—" The words caught in her throat. "It's like doing this balancing act, without a net."

His eyes widened as the realization hit him. Reaching across the table, he covered her trembling hands. "I wasn't trying to take anything away from you, Whit. That wasn't my intention. I sell houses every day, so it never occurred to me…"

"I know," she said too quickly. "I just felt obligated to tell you why I hit the panic button. Go ahead and sell the condo. I'll deal with it, no matter what happens."

No one in their household was the same after that argument.

Logan took Whitney at her word, and immediately went ahead with the sale of the condo. Yet he berated himself every step of the way. He was so angry with himself, he couldn't see straight. He should have known, he should have realized. Whitney had been shifted from pillar to post as a child, it made sense that she wanted to salvage her only refuge. He should have asked, not told. He should have supported her, not insisted they do the logical thing and sell off everything she'd worked for. Instead he'd tossed down the gauntlet and offered her the opportunity to walk away if things didn't suit her.

After he'd done that, he knew how much he needed her. He was finally ready to move forward with his life and open his heart again, but he was beginning to second guess Whitney's true desires.

He had intentionally accepted the offer on the condo because he didn't want to give her an escape route; something inside him wanted to make her stay with him, forever and ever. To lessen his guilt, he told her that he'd make up the difference she expected for the condo. But she waved it off, saying it wasn't important.

The gesture made him determined to set things right.

Then she matter-of-factly said she'd thought about it, and realized what was important and what wasn't.

That was his undoing: he began to wonder just how important he was. The hell of it was, he wanted to be the most important thing in her life. And, after he set the date to close on the condo, he doubted that he was.

Whitney's heart was so heavy that she felt dead and dull inside. She thought she'd self-destruct from the sheer weight of her worries. It was inconceivable to her that she'd lashed out at Logan over something as stupid as the condo. It was nothing, a nondescript residence, in a blue-collar neighborhood. Sure, it was her little bit of heaven, but she couldn't fathom why she'd jeopardize her life with Logan and Amanda to save it.

Perhaps the past had caught up with her. Nagging memories of her childhood fears, coupled with the pain of her first marriage—the bills, the quickie divorce, and coarse behavior she'd endured—made her reluctant to be financially, or even emotionally, dependent on Logan.

Logan wasn't responsible for her mother's defection, or poor parenting skills. He had no idea how bad it was, or how deeply Whitney feared being abandoned—or how desperately she wanted to be loved. She'd always glossed over that first part of her life, mostly because she didn't want her peers to know, later because she tried not to dwell on it. She'd tried to convince herself that she could go on and rise above it.

Now it was coming back to haunt her.

Suddenly her life, and the choices she'd made, made sense, and the knowledge came to her like the wheels clicking in on a slot machine. Her marriage at eighteen to Kevin was nothing more than an alliance to stave off the loneliness and the rejection.

Logan was not like Kevin. He was a man of integrity and he'd proven it to her daily. He treated her with respect and he loved his child with his whole heart. He was kind and tolerant of his parents even though he had his own idea of family. He was honest in his business dealings and generous to friends. He didn't abuse the assets life had given him, but shared his health, wealth and wisdom without reservation.

Logan Monroe was everything she'd ever idealized in a man.

He was her husband, her partner and friend. She loved him, unequivocally.

Whitney had two choices: she could either accept things the way they were or she could throw them all away. If she accepted them, she'd also have to accept the fact that in their marriage, love could be a one-way street. For Logan could never possibly love her, not the way she loved him.

It may well be that Logan could never possibly love her at all.

Chapter Fifteen

The adoption promised to be an informal proceeding at the Melville County Courthouse—but it was hanging over their heads, and constantly on their minds. The case was assigned to Judge Miles, and he had a reputation for being quite an unpredictable, crusty old character. Madeline arranged to meet them at the courthouse.

Whitney smoothed the skirt of her sleeveless dress and adjusted the jacket as she looked out the window. She wore the bracelet Logan had given her and guessed it was too much. But she needed it with her, so she could touch it and be reassured. "It's too bad your folks couldn't come," she said idly.

"To be expected," Logan said.

He had been unusually quiet since their fight, and Whitney found it deeply disturbing. She couldn't imagine he was still angry, that would be unlike Logan, but she worried she had driven the wedge too deep. She knew, eventually, they would have to talk and come to terms with the why's and how's of their relationship.

"Still…I know you'd like to have them here," she said, smiling sadly over at him.

His eyes flickered to the side window, to check the up-coming intersection. "Yeah, well, it's odd what people think is important in life, isn't it?"

Whitney regretfully thought of the condo. "I mentioned they should come over after work to celebrate. I hope that's okay."

He nodded and pulled into the parking lot adjacent to the courthouse. "Of course. Sometimes you just gotta take 'em when you can get 'em, right?" He pulled the car into the first available parking spot and gazed over at her, his eyes unreadable.

Whitney reached over and patted his forearm. "It's going to be okay," she said softly, so Amanda couldn't hear her. "This is what we've been waiting for."

Logan didn't reply. He opened the car door, then stepped out to open the back door for Amanda. Whitney joined them at the fender of the car, pausing long enough to straighten the denim skirt of Amanda's bibbed jumper. She flounced the bow in her hair more as a gesture of love than necessity.

In response, Amanda tucked one hand into Whitney's and one hand into Logan's and, skipping between them, led them straight to the courthouse steps. Madeline was waiting for them at the top.

"We're in the family court at the end of the hall," she said, walking ahead.

Whitney's palms went moist and her shoulders tightened. She couldn't bear to look at Logan, she could only con-centrate on putting one step in front of the other. What was the matter with her? This should be the easy part. Once everything was signed, sealed, and Amanda was safely "delivered," her transition into family life would be com-plete.

The courtroom was not what Whitney expected and she sank into the leather chair Madeline indicated. Whitney,

Amanda, Logan, and Madeline, sat in a line at the conference table, all facing the honeyed oak bench where Judge Miles would sit. A court clerk came in to shuffle papers with Madeline and whisper to her.

Amanda squirmed in her chair and Logan checked his wristwatch against the industrial-strength clock hanging on the south wall. Whitney had the uncanny sense she was under surveillance, as if Judge Miles was looking out on them from some two-way mirror, deciding whether or not they could be good parents. Her heart tripped double-time.

At the clerk's instruction, they stood when the judge entered the chambers. His smile was plastic, his sharp eyes pinning them as he sat. Heaving a big sigh, he adjusted his robes and trailed a glance over the sheaf of papers before him. "After reviewing the caseworker's recommendations," he announced without ceremony, "I'd like to talk to Amanda, please." Beside her, Whitney felt Amanda straighten. "You must be Amanda," he said, softening his tone. "Well, I usually don't do this, but I'd like to have you come up here, in this big chair beside me, so we can talk for a few minutes. Can you do that?"

Amanda nodded and stood up, and the clerk opened the door to the witness stand so Amanda could slide into the chair. Whitney shot a wary glance to Logan. His expression remained impassive.

"So you know why you're here, don't you, Amanda?" She nodded. "Your dad and mom want to adopt you, and make you their little girl."

Amanda wiggled, uncomfortably. "I know…but…"

"Yes?"

"I don't call her my mom, though. I call her Whitney."

Judge Miles's eyebrows raised, like antennae. "Really?"

"My mom, the first one who was going to adopt me, died. My dad just married Whitney, not long ago, so she said it's okay if I call her Whitney."

"Okay…." The judge nodded thoughtfully. "I can see that I don't have to tell you to tell the truth when you're up here. Or that I need you to tell me the truth about how you feel about living with your dad and…Whitney.''

Amanda nodded earnestly.

"So, are there any other kids living in your house with you?"

"Nope, just me. I'm the only one."

The judge seemed fascinated by his reading glasses, and flexed the bows thoughtfully between his fingers. "I see. Tell me about your dad," he said.

"I've lived with him almost for forever. Since before I can remember."

"That long?"

"He said that since he and my first mom couldn't have their own little girl, he got me instead."

"Really?" Judge Miles sat back, swiveling to frown at Logan. "Like replaceable parts?"

Logan's shoulder's drooped and he started to say something, but Madeline put a hand on his arm to quiet him.

"He works an awful lot. Real hard. But he has to, 'cause Grandma and Grandpa talk to him about it, and tell him what he has to do. It's all they ever talk about."

Judge Miles lifted his head, considering. "I see. So he's not home very much. Well. That's interesting. Now…tell me about Whitney."

"She's pretty funny."

"Really? Is she funny all the time?"

"No. Sometimes she gets sad, like when she talks about how her mom left her."

Whitney cringed and her chest started to hurt.

The judge, with Amanda's help, was making them look like the most dysfunctional family on the face of the earth.

"Yes…" Judge Miles flipped over some paperwork, then glanced at Madeline. "I think there was some reference made to her being raised by her grandmother." Madeline smiled and nodded firmly, as if the paperwork was correct. "Well, Amanda…tell me…how do you like living in your house with your dad and Whitney?"

Amanda hesitated, she nibbled her lower lip and frowned. "Well..." she said finally, "I've been thinking a lot about that, and I've decided I'd rather not live there."

"Excuse me?"

"I don't want to live in the house anymore. Not if it makes Daddy and Whitney fight." Logan uttered an expletive under his breath and, save for her jaw dropping, Whitney sat motionless. "Daddy sold Whitney's condo," she confided, leaning forward, "and I think it made Whitney cry."

"Ah, I see," Judge Miles said, though it was apparent he didn't see at all. "Tell me. What do you think about all this?"

Amanda hesitated, her mouth pursing like a taut little rosebud before she spit out the answer. "I think Daddy should give it back. Or else he should sell his house, too. 'Cause he always said 'fair's fair.' If they wanted, they could come live in my playhouse with me. That would really be okay. Because we always have a great time together."

Amanda's ultimate solution made the judge chuckle, and as he wiped his eyes his belly shook beneath his black robes. "Yes, well, that would be something to consider. I'll tell you what...I want to talk to you some more, but I'd like to talk to Whitney now. Ask her about this condo fiasco. So you can step down, thank you."

While Amanda took her seat at the table, Judge Miles turned on Whitney with all the aplomb of a man who wanted to see her squirm. "Whitney, I hear you sold your condo." He waited expectantly for her answer.

"Yes." Under the table, she worried the button on her jacket. "It needed some work, and I thought maybe we should wait to sell it, so there was some discussion about that. I think that is what Amanda means. But Logan found a buyer, and...so we did. Sell it, I mean."

"I get the distinct impression you didn't want to sell it."

In this courtroom, Whitney knew she was under oath.

She had to tell the truth; there was no skirting the ghosts of her past. "My mother left me in the care of my grandmother when I was young, Your Honor. Because of that, my home has always been very important to me, and I attach a lot of feelings to it. When Logan told me he had a buyer for it, I overreacted. I'm ashamed to say that I got my priorities mixed up." She looked down, guiltily, as if she were exposing her deepest sins. "I've since realized, Your Honor, that it's not the feelings I have for the *things* in my life. It's not the condo. It's not my business. It's the feelings I have for the *people* in my life that's the most important. My feelings for Logan, and Amanda."

"And you've explained that to Amanda?"

Whitney traced the bracelet, wishing it would give her the strength she needed to get through this ordeal. "Perhaps not in so many words," she said quietly.

"Perhaps you should." Judge Miles tilted back in his chair. "According to the information the caseworker, Madeline Enright, provided me with, you married Mr. Monroe recently." He paused. "Why?"

Whitney stalled, fully aware her emotions would be flayed raw by the time this adoption hearing was over. She had to do what was best for Logan—and she had to tell the truth. "Because it seemed like the right thing to do at the time...especially when you love someone. You want to share your life with them."

"You love Logan Monroe?"

"I do, Your Honor. I love him very, very much."

Judge Miles lifted his bushy brows and clucked, before thumping forward in his chair. "And I don't have to ask how you feel about Amanda. What's not to love about her, right?" Whitney smiled weakly. "Mr. Monroe," he went on, "I have to tell you that this is the first time in my entire career, I have ever had a child say they didn't want to live in their house, then suggest the whole family run away to the playhouse."

"It's come as a shock to us, too, Your Honor," Logan

said, trying to smile. "This is the first we've heard about it."

"Mmm," Judge Miles replied, his eyes scanning the paperwork before him.

"Your Honor? If I may?" Logan said. "Whitney and I don't fight, exactly. But the issue of the condo was difficult. I didn't understand what it meant to Whitney, and—" he shrugged "—I've had time to think it over, and I've come to the conclusion it would be best to sell my house, too. Like Amanda's said, 'fair's fair.' I've formulated a listing, and you're welcome to take a look at it." Logan extended the paper across the table.

Judge Miles disdainfully waved it away. "Not interested," he said.

"I want to do the right thing for my family, Your Honor. I realized it might be best for all of us to have a fresh start. If that means giving up my home—I mean, our home."

"Is it your desire, sir, to go live in the playhouse?" Before Logan could answer the taunt, the judge rose. "We obviously have some issues to explore. Miss Enright, I'd like to have you and Amanda retire to chambers with me. Immediately."

There was nothing but dead silence after Judge Miles swept from his courtroom. Whitney was torn between wailing and railing. "This doesn't look good, does it?" She stared straight ahead at the Tennessee State Seal hanging over the bench.

"I'd say not." Logan leaned back in the chair, and slipped both hands into his pants' pockets. "It started out bad, and just kept going downhill from there. But never, not in my wildest dreams, did I ever think Amanda would say something like that about living with us. Or not living with us. Whatever the case may be."

"She didn't mean it, Logan. Not like that. But we scared her. My insecurities made her insecure. It's my fault. I let the condo thing get out of control."

"Forget that," he said, waving off the blame. "I should

have thought about how much it meant to you. Since I do this for a business, it's routine for me. People move on. Then when I started writing the listing for my place, and all the memories came flooding back..." He let the sentence hang, unfinished. He stared off into space. "People move on..." he repeated, as if he were talking to himself.

"I can't believe you thought selling your house would fix everything," she said, "because it won't. Not for me. I love it there, Logan. You've made me feel like I belong. I've never once felt like it wasn't the right thing to do. Maybe the adjustment has been far harder on you than me. I know it's hard to make changes, but—"

He turned to her, his left arm slipping over the back of her chair as he twined the fingers of his right hand through hers. "It would have been harder, Whit, if it wasn't for you. It's like there're two parts of my life, the before and after, with Amanda being right smack-dab in the center, keeping it all together."

Whitney stared at him, both cherishing his words and loathing them. She wished, desperately, that she could be the one at the center of his life. Yet he'd given her credit for being there for him. "It's all going to fall apart, isn't it?" she whispered.

"Well, right now, it looks like one muddled adoption," he conceded.

"I just get my family, only to lose it." Taking a long, shaky breath, she steadied herself against his shoulder.

Logan moved closer, shielding her, his forehead grazing her temple. "No matter what happens, I can't thank you enough," he whispered. "For trying to salvage everything, for what you said today."

Her eyes smarted, and she convulsively swallowed. She was going to lose everything. Logan. Amanda. Her marriage. All the hopes, the dreams. "I only told the truth, Logan."

He hesitated. "Even about loving me?"

"Particularly about loving you." She gave him a watery

smile, her lips quivering uncontrollably. "Logan, you fool. You big jock, you. I've been in love with you since tenth grade. And then you have to go and ask me to marry you. Like it's a favor. And I sleep in your bed, and…"

"Whit?" He stroked her shoulder. "Are you crying?"

"No," she lied. "It's just that telling the truth hurts so doggone much it makes my eyes sweat." He chuckled sympathetically and his arm tightened around her.

"Whit? No matter what happens today, we'll work this out."

She gazed up at him, willing him to say the words she needed to hear.

Instead a smile reached his eyes, making the corners crinkle. "You've been wonderful, through all of this. You're the perfect wife, and friend…and…lover."

"Logan…" Her fingers curled around the lapels of his suit, pulling him closer. "Maybe I should have told you sooner, instead of wasting all those weeks…I should have have taken the chance, and risked—"

"Shh," he soothed. "Don't say that. I don't regret any of the way our life came together. It just wasn't the ordinary way. Whatever happens, we'll get through it."

"Logan, I just love you…" Whitney's eyelids pricked, and she could barely utter the words; she felt so deeply, it anguished her. "So much…and I need…"

The door to Judge Miles's chambers opened and the clerk cleared her throat. Logan and Whitney broke apart, guiltily. Judge Miles entered, and when Whitney looked up she could have sworn she saw his mouth twitch. He sat down and waited patiently for Madeline to take her place while Amanda plopped back into the seat next to them.

"We have a little problem here," Judge Miles began bluntly. "I've just learned that the playhouse is located on the piece of property on which you are now residing."

Both Logan and Whitney nodded dumbly. Neither could believe their ears.

"Considering that, and provided you sell your current

home, Mr. Monroe, I can see where the three of you could wind up homeless.'' He paused, smiling through the emphasis. ''Of course, you'd be together...and I guess that's the point of this. I'd recommend you sit down and discuss your options.'' He laughed heartily. ''I will tell you Mr. and Mrs. Monroe, I have never had a situation where every member of the household willingly sacrifices their home, in one way or another, just so they can be together. Amanda endorses your character, Miss Enright endorses your character and I have no reason to doubt this adoption will be a success.'' He leaned over the bench to Amanda. ''Ready?'' he asked, offering his gavel, handle end first. ''Now, hit it! Right here!''

Amanda proudly stood up, walked to the bench and banged the gavel soundly on the spot he indicated.

''Adoption granted,'' he declared.

Chapter Sixteen

Logan and Whitney and Amanda talked and laughed the whole way home.

"Now my name's Monroe, just like yours," Amanda said triumphantly. "The judge said."

"And just what did you talk about in his chambers," Logan asked. "I want to know."

"Oh, he asked if Whitney was as nice as she looked— and, of course, I said yes. And I told him you were the best dad in the whole world. And then he said we should get a puppy—"

"*A what?*" Both Logan and Whitney asked in unison, turning to look over the seat at Amanda. Logan accidentally turned the wheel and Whitney grabbed for the armrest.

"He said puppies make a family real. He said a black Labrador was best. And then he made me repeat it, to make sure I got it right."

Logan and Whitney sat back, then they exchanged glances. She bubbled over with laughter; he did the same.

"I'm not sure there'll be room in the playhouse," he finally muttered. "Those are big dogs."

Whitney smiled so hard her cheeks hurt. "Amanda..," she said, "about where we're living? I know your daddy told the judge today that he was thinking about selling the house and starting over, but I don't think we need to do that. I like where I'm living…and you have your friends and your school. I think we could be really happy, just staying here."

Amanda considered, soberly, as Logan turned into the driveway.

"We talked about it, Amanda," Logan said. "And I told Whitney that I feel like my life is in parts, the before and after part, with you in the middle, bridging all the gaps. But Whitney's the 'after' part. The 'happily ever after' part."

Logan's declaration surprised her, and Whitney's throat swelled with emotion. She couldn't trust herself to answer. Reaching for Logan's hand instead, she threaded her fingers through his. If he could only tell her he loved her, her happiness would be complete. Perhaps this was the compromise she'd have to make.

"I guess it's okay." Amanda, apparently satisfied that the issue had been resolved, reached across their intertwined hands and pointed to the porch. "What's that?"

Both Logan and Whitney looked up. Huge packing boxes were stacked hodgepodge by the front door.

Logan grimaced, pulled up in front and shut off the ignition. "I'm calling the post office. I just hate it when they leave stuff like that."

"Maybe it isn't the post office," Whitney said, getting out of the car and shutting the door after Amanda. "Maybe it's something from—" Amanda was already on the landing, trying to lift one of the boxes.

"These really aren't heavy," she called.

Logan joined her, easing the box away from her before it tumbled out of her grasp and down the steps. Whitney checked the return address. "Oh my," she said. "I think we need to take these inside and check them out."

Within minutes, packing paper was strewn all over the library. "It's Argus," Amanda screeched, happily pulling the beloved teddy to her chest. "Oh, my gosh! How many Arguses are there?"

Whitney smiled like a Cheshire cat. "About seventy-two, give or take a few. I figured it was best to take the whole lot, just to cover my bases."

"You found him, Whit," Logan said, his voice filled with disbelief as he pulled another teddy from the box. "You never gave up."

"I told you I'd find him," Whitney said. "I promised."

Logan pulled out a second teddy and perched one on each knee, studying the pair. "You promised. And you never gave up on this bear—or on me," he said quietly, his eyes filled with awe, appreciation.

"It's really how your daddy and I met again, Amanda," Whitney said carefully, refusing to take credit for Logan's teddy bear quest. "He wanted to replace Argus for you."

Logan shook his head, musing. "You know, pip, you named this teddy bear Argus right after you came to live in this house. I thought you named him by accident, but do you know what Argus means?"

"No."

"I looked it up one day." He tweaked the bear's ear, then ran a fingertip over his black button nose. "It means watchful guardian. I think he's been watching over you— and maybe me, too—whether we realized it or not. It's strange for Argus to come back into our lives again, particularly on such a momentous day, isn't it?"

Whitney's heart turned over. She knew what Logan was thinking, without having to guess. He was considering the "before" part of his life—and for one brief millisecond she wondered if he was truly ready to move on—or if the reminders of his late wife would keep dragging him back.

"Who was that?" Whitney asked as Logan hung up the phone.

"My folks. They're coming over and want to go out for ice cream, to celebrate the adoption."

"Oh." Whitney stopped and looked down at her blouse. "Maybe I better change, then. I know they like that place over on Miller."

"Don't bother. We're not invited."

"No?"

"It was sort of my doing. I had something I wanted to show you and I said maybe they'd like to spend some quality time with their new granddaughter. They called on the cell phone, so they'll be here in five minutes."

"Quality time," she repeated. "I like that. Will this be a new phrase for your folks?"

"Looks like it," he said, inclining his head. "I don't know. Maybe from what Mom said, they were just so afraid of us losing Amanda that they wanted to distance themselves from her. To save us, to save themselves."

Whitney stared at him, aching for his love, his devotion. "I know the feeling," she said finally, unable to drive the sadness from her smile.

Whitney had Amanda dressed and out the door with her grandparents in record time.

"Come on. Let's go for a walk," Logan suggested after they left.

"A walk?" she asked, mildly disappointed. She'd come to cherish the moments when Logan wrapped his arms around her, when they made love and he lost himself inside her. She'd hoped they could take some time, some intimate time, together.

"Come on," he said, holding the back door open. "If you hurry, we'll still get a glimpse of the sunset."

"Logan," she said carefully, "I feel like this is really the first day of my life with you. I want to savor it, I don't want to rush through it."

He laughed and closed the door after them. They tarried for a few minutes on the beach, letting the sun sink down into a red-pink haze that rippled over the water. Dusk enveloped them, and he threw an arm around her shoulders. "Tomorrow, I need to get some paint and finish that playhouse." He moved her in that direction, to the beautiful little playhouse where Amanda spent endless, happy hours.

They paused before the gingerbread facade, both smiling as they recalled what had happened in court that afternoon.

Logan stooped, stepping onto the front porch. "Come into my abode, Mrs. Monroe," he invited, pushing open the pint-size door. "Our daughter is certain that we can live here, in this storybook house, happily, and forever and ever."

Whitney stood stock-still, taking in the scene. Inside, the tiny rooms were filled with teddy bears and roses. Dozens and dozens of roses. Arguses occupied every spare corner, and every surface. A hurricane lamp was centered on the middle of the tiny play table, and candlelight flickered from within the glass. Beside it was a bottle of champagne, chilling on ice, and two stemmed flutes.

"Oh, Logan. How? How did you manage this?"

"You may be creative and clever, but," he said modestly, "I have my ingenious moments. Particularly when it comes to the woman in my life."

The way he said it crimped a corner of her heart. Whitney tried to convince herself it was his way of saying he loved her. She needed more than anything to believe that.

Allowing him to hold the door for her, she sat on the tiny chair, her knees bumping the table. The scent of roses filled the room. She caressed the petals of those on the table, tracing a fingernail over the curled edges.

Logan carefully eased onto the chair next to her. "Whitney? Remember when we told Amanda that we were getting married? And I had the engagement ring, and she helped me slip it onto your finger?"

Whitney automatically fingered the diamond. "Yes...?"

"It was just a beginning, Whitney. From both of us." He reached into his pants' pocket. "I realized today that I wanted you to have something just from me." Lifting her hand, he slipped a circle of gold and diamonds just past her first knuckle, fourth finger. "It's an eternity ring," he said unnecessarily, "because I'll always love you."

Whitney gasped, the sharp intake of air causing a deep, radiating pain behind her breastbone.

"I love you, Whitney," he repeated. "I love everything about you. It's not only your patience or your sense of humor. It's the little things. The way you squish the sand between your toes when we walk on the beach. The way you laugh when you tell knock-knock jokes with Amanda. I even love the way you make pineapple upside-down cake...but I like it best when we share it—one plate and two forks." His eyes grew soft, even luminous in the candlelight. "At night, I watch you read to Amanda, and think it is the most precious sight I'll ever be privileged to witness. My wife, and my daughter. Together. You made me love again, Whitney. You made me realize it was possible to have a second chance at happiness. I could never begin to tell you how much it all means to me."

One tear dribbled from the corner of Whitney's eye. She swiped at it, then pushed the ring all the way onto her finger, sniffling as she coupled it with her wedding rings. "I love you, too," she said, her voice cracking with emotion.

"It was the best I could do on the spur of the moment," he said awkwardly. "If you don't like it, or—"

"Oh, Logan. Don't say that. I've never had anything mean so much."

"It may be a notch above junk jewelry, Whit," he said, dismissing the token, "but it's still a thing. What counts is in here—" he took her hand and held it against his chest "—in my heart. You own it. This is really your home. It's filled with love and happiness, and it's where you've come to live."

Beneath her palm, his heart hammered out a wild, staccatoed rhythm.

"Logan Monroe...," she whispered, "what have you

done to me? I've loved you for forever, and then you had to go and marry me, and make me love you even more. You treat me so wonderfully, and you make me feel so special, and you shower me with gifts." She glanced regretfully down at the ring. "I can only give you my love, it's the only thing I have to give you."

"Your love?" he asked incredulously. "Whitney, it's all I'll ever want. It's the most valuable thing of all." He leaned over and traced a finger down her cheek and onto her lips.

She instinctively kissed his fingertips, wanting to draw him closer and into herself. Her mouth felt bare, naked, when he moved his hand away to cup the back of her neck. But when he kissed her, she experienced passion, and a deep, overwhelming sense of commitment.

"I feel like I have to keep saying it," he whispered against her mouth, "because I want you to know it, and believe it. I love you, Whitney, and I'll honor you always."

"I like the 'always' part," she whispered back. "We'll always be a family, always with love to share."

* * * * *

If you enjoyed what you just read,
then we've got an offer you can't resist!

Take 2 bestselling love stories FREE!

Plus get a FREE surprise gift!

Clip this page and mail it to Silhouette Reader Service™

IN U.S.A.	IN CANADA
3010 Walden Ave.	P.O. Box 609
P.O. Box 1867	Fort Erie, Ontario
Buffalo, N.Y. 14240-1867	L2A 5X3

YES! Please send me 2 free Silhouette Romance® novels and my free surprise gift. After receiving them, if I don't wish to receive anymore, I can return the shipping statement marked cancel. If I don't cancel, I will receive 6 brand-new novels every month, before they're available in stores! In the U.S.A., bill me at the bargain price of $3.15 plus 25¢ shipping and handling per book and applicable sales tax, if any*. In Canada, bill me at the bargain price of $3.50 plus 25¢ shipping and handling per book and applicable taxes**. That's the complete price and a savings of at least 10% off the cover prices—what a great deal! I understand that accepting the 2 free books and gift places me under no obligation ever to buy any books. I can always return a shipment and cancel at any time. Even if I never buy another book from Silhouette, the 2 free books and gift are mine to keep forever.

215 SEN DFNQ
315 SEN DFNR

Name	(PLEASE PRINT)	
Address	Apt.#	
City	State/Prov.	Zip/Postal Code

* Terms and prices subject to change without notice. Sales tax applicable in N.Y.
** Canadian residents will be charged applicable provincial taxes and GST.
  All orders subject to approval. Offer limited to one per household and not valid to
  current Silhouette Romance® subscribers.
® are registered trademarks of Harlequin Enterprises Limited.

SROM01   ©1998 Harlequin Enterprises Limited

SILHOUETTE®
MAKES YOU
A STAR!

Feel like a star with Silhouette.

We will fly you and a guest to New York City for an exciting weekend stay at a glamorous 5-star hotel. Experience a refreshing day at one of New York's trendiest spas and have your photo taken by a professional. Plus, receive $1,000 U.S. spending money!

Flowers...long walks...dinner for two... how does Silhouette Books make romance come alive for you?

Send us a script, with 500 words or less, along with visuals (only drawings, magazine cutouts or photographs or combination thereof). Show us how Silhouette Makes Your Love Come Alive. Be creative and have fun. No purchase necessary. All entries must be clearly marked with your name, address and telephone number. All entries will become property of Silhouette and are not returnable. **Contest closes September 28, 2001.**

Please send your entry to: **Silhouette Makes You a Star!**

In U.S.A.
P.O. Box 9069
Buffalo, NY, 14269-9069

In Canada
P.O. Box 637
Fort Erie, ON, L2A 5X3

Look for contest details on the next page, by visiting www.eHarlequin.com or request a copy by sending a self-addressed envelope to the applicable address above. Contest open to Canadian and U.S. residents who are 18 or over. Void where prohibited.

Silhouette®
Where love comes alive™

Our lucky winner's photo will appear in a Silhouette ad. Join the fun!

SRMYAS1

HARLEQUIN "SILHOUETTE MAKES YOU A STAR!" CONTEST 1308
OFFICIAL RULES
NO PURCHASE NECESSARY TO ENTER

1. To enter, follow directions published in the offer to which you are responding. Contest begins June 1, 2001, and ends on September 28, 2001. Entries must be postmarked by September 28, 2001, and received by October 5, 2001. Enter by hand-printing (or typing) on an 8 ½" x 11" piece of paper your name, address (including zip code), contest number/name and attaching a script containing <u>500 words or less, along with drawings, photographs or magazine cutouts, or combinations thereof</u> (i.e., collage) <u>on no larger than 9" x 12"</u> piece of paper, describing how the <u>Silhouette books make romance come alive for you.</u> Mail via first-class mail to: Harlequin "Silhouette Makes You a Star!" Contest 1308, (in the U.S.) P.O. Box 9069, Buffalo, NY 14269-9069, (in Canada) P.O. Box 637, Fort Erie, Ontario, Canada L2A 5X3. Limit one entry per person, household or organization.

2. Contests will be judged by a panel of members of the Harlequin editorial, marketing and public relations staff. Fifty percent of criteria will be judged against script and fifty percent will be judged against drawing, photographs and/or magazine cutouts. Judging criteria will be based on the following:

   - Sincerity—25%
   - Originality and Creativity—50%
   - Emotionally Compelling—25%

   In the event of a tie, duplicate prizes will be awarded. Decisions of the judges are final.

3. All entries become the property of Torstar Corp. and may be used for future promotional purposes. Entries will not be returned. No responsibility is assumed for lost, late, illegible, incomplete, inaccurate, nondelivered or misdirected mail.

4. Contest open only to residents of the U.S. <u>(except Puerto Rico)</u> and Canada who are 18 years of age or older, and is void wherever prohibited by law; all applicable laws and regulations apply. Any litigation within the Province of Quebec respecting the conduct or organization of a publicity contest may be submitted to the Régie des alcools, des courses et des jeux for a ruling. Any litigation respecting the awarding of a prize may be submitted to the Régie des alcools, des courses et des jeux only for the purpose of helping the parties reach a settlement. Employees and immediate family members of Torstar Corp. and D. L. Blair, Inc., their affiliates, subsidiaries and all other agencies, entities and persons connected with the use, marketing or conduct of this contest are not eligible to enter. Taxes on prizes are the sole responsibility of the winner. Acceptance of any prize offered constitutes permission to use winner's name, photograph or other likeness for the purposes of advertising, trade and promotion on behalf of Torstar Corp., its affiliates and subsidiaries without further compensation to the winner, unless prohibited by law.

5. Winner will be determined no later than November 30, 2001, and will be notified by mail. Winner will be required to sign and return an Affidavit of Eligibility/Release of Liability/Publicity Release form within 15 days after winner notification. Noncompliance within that time period may result in disqualification and an alternative winner may be selected. All travelers must execute a Release of Liability prior to ticketing and must possess required travel documents (e.g., passport, photo ID) where applicable. Trip must be booked by December 31, 2001, and completed within one year of notification. No substitution of prize permitted by winner. Torstar Corp. and D. L. Blair, Inc., their parents, affiliates and subsidiaries are not responsible for errors in printing of contest, entries and/or game pieces. In the event of printing or other errors that may result in unintended prize values or duplication of prizes, all affected game pieces or entries shall be null and void. **Purchase or acceptance of a product offer does not improve your chances of winning.**

6. Prizes: (1) Grand Prize—A 2-night/3-day trip for two (2) to New York City, including round-trip coach air transportation nearest winner's home and hotel accommodations (double occupancy) at The Plaza Hotel, a glamorous afternoon makeover at <u>a trendy New York spa</u>, $1,000 in U.S. spending money and an opportunity to <u>have a professional photo taken and appear in a Silhouette advertisement</u> (approximate retail value: $7,000). (10) Ten Runner-Up Prizes of gift packages (retail value $50 ea.). Prizes consist of only those items listed as part of the prize. Limit one prize per person. Prize is valued in U.S. currency.

7. For the name of the winner (available after December 31, 2001) send a self-addressed, stamped envelope to: Harlequin "Silhouette Makes You a Star!" Contest 1197 Winners, P.O. Box 4200 Blair, NE 68009-4200 or you may access the www.eHarlequin.com Web site through February 28, 2002.

Contest sponsored by Torstar Corp., P.O Box 9042, Buffalo, NY 14269-9042.

SRMYAS2

SILHOUETTE *Romance*

COMING NEXT MONTH

RSCNM0901